BACK FROM HELL

MARINE FOR YOU: BOOK TWO

MARISSA DOBSON

DEDICATION

Back from Hell is for everyone who has suffered with depression or PTSD. It's a tough road to travel and there will be many times when you will feel alone. But, know that you're not. There are people behind you, supporting you every step of the way. There's no shame in reaching out for help. Stay strong and fight the demons that haunt you. In the end, you'll be stronger for it. Never give up!

Believe in your dreams, chase them with everything you have, and when it gets lonely or hard, remember what you're fighting for. Have faith because in the end it will be worth it. We're behind you, supporting you at every crossroads.

ACKNOWLEDGEMENT

I would like to take a moment to thank everyone who helped me make *Back from Hell* happen. This journey started with Rosa Sophia who, while editing *Lucky Chance*, said she could feel a good story coming from Kyle. Before her suggestion of giving him his own story I hadn't planned to write it. Now, I couldn't be happier. Kyle's story came alive for me and brought home the struggles some of our military men and women come home with. We must never forget that they volunteered for their service to keep those of us at home safe and free. They deserve our utmost respect and appreciation.

Thank you, Dana Michelle Burnett, who took time out of her busy schedule to answer some questions on amputations and prosthesis. Also, thank you Lynn Peters for your help with the military healthcare side of *Back from Hell*.

I also would like to thank Teresa Riley, Allyson Brann, and my street team Marissa's Dreamweavers, my amazing editors/proofreaders: Molly Daniels, Natalie Owens, and Brynna Curry.

Last but certainly not least, I would like to thank my amazing husband, Thomas. Those of you who read the dedications and acknowledgements of my books will see that he is mentioned in each of them. That's because he is my biggest support. I don't know if I would have ever published my first book without him. He's incredible and I couldn't have asked for a better soulmate. I love you, Thomas.

PART ONE

Chapter One

Kyle Phillips lay in a hospital bed with his eyes closed so he didn't have to look at what had become of his body. If he stayed that way, he could try to forget he'd lost a leg and arm in that IED explosion, leaving him half the man he was before. The burns along half of his body proved harder to forget. The pain down his side would not be denied.

Surgery after surgery helped to repair the damage left behind. That torturous experience had only done so much in returning him to the man he was before. There would always be scars along his face and body. Too many times he heard he should be thankful he was alive, while all the time he wished he had died overseas. It would have been better than living as a freak.

Gunnery Sergeant Lucky Diamond had left after Kyle refused to acknowledge the man who had been in charge of the fateful mission that left him so disfigured. How could he look his Gunnery Sergeant in the eyes, when he had failed? He was the one that handed the information to his Gunny and it not only left him in this state but had also gotten Weber killed.

Weber. A tear rolled down his cheek for his brother in arms. They graduated boot camp together and this had been their first deployment. A deployment that Weber never came back from. If either of them had known, would they have decided to do something besides join the military once they graduated high school? Or would the fact they did ultimately bring down their target outweigh the loss they had encountered? Gunnery Sergeant Diamond might blame himself, but it was nothing like the guilt Kyle carried.

He'd carry that guilt for the rest of his days, but it wouldn't change anything. He'd lost his friend and that hurt more than his own disfigurement. He and Weber had bonded over their training, encouraging each other through the worst parts, and now, when he needed his friend the most, he wasn't here. The loss pained him more than the loss of his limbs.

"I'd rather be where you are, Weber."

"Need something, Private First Class Phillips?" Brenda, the older day nurse, stood in his doorway. "I heard you talking to yourself. We have people who are paid to listen. Shall I get someone for you? Talking to thin air doesn't help much."

"No, thanks. I'm fine. Unless you can get me a bottle of whiskey."

"You know the rules. If you start working with your physical therapist, you'll be out of here in no time."

He tipped his head to the side and glared at her. Even with the anger, it was hard to be mad at someone who looked so much like someone's grandmother. All he wanted to do was get out of this place, but he wouldn't be able to do that until he learned to walk with his damn prosthesis and use the prosthetic arm. Physical therapy was the last thing he wanted. Every time he did those damn things, he was reminded he would never be whole again. The prosthesis might make him appear more normal, especially when he had long sleeves and pants, but all it did was hide reality.

When he lay in bed, he could keep his eyes closed and, with the phantom pains, it was almost as if he still had his limbs. The pains might be agonizing but, in those brief moments, he could pretend he was whole. Yet, the minute he opened his eyes, there was no more pretending. Nothing could hide the way the sheets fell flat just below the knee, or the fact his arm was gone from just below the elbow. His doctors tried to reassure him that, with the aid of his prosthesis, he could live a normal life. *Normal life.* Who would want to spend the rest of their life with a man who couldn't even hold them without the aid of some manmade arm?

"Remember we're only here to help. We want to see you regain your life."

Her words brought him back out of his thoughts for a moment and he watched her continue down the hallway. If they wanted to help him, they should just let him die. *Damn it Gunny, you should have let me die.* His earlier words rang through his thoughts. Even after the pain in Gunnery Sergeant Diamond's eyes, Kyle still didn't regret them. He wished he were dead rather than have to deal with this. He wasn't sure how to face the world again. Or even what to do with his life now. *What do I have to offer to anyone anymore?*

He glanced around the room and the need to get out of there rose within him. He didn't know where he'd go. He'd need aftercare and, as a foster child, he had no family to fall back on. His last foster family sent occasional letters to him but there was no chance he could stay with them while he figured out what to do with his life. Even his girlfriend of over two years had abandoned him. She couldn't deal with how he looked now.

"How did I miss how shallow she was?" The answer was as clear as his missing limbs. He'd overlooked it because he didn't want to see the truth. He wanted to enjoy the time they had together instead of thinking about their fights every time he put his military service before her. The biggest fight had happened just hours before he deployed. She wanted a serviceman on her arm because of *how good they looked in uniform*, her words, but she didn't want to deal with everything else that came along with it. He was naïve to think that with time she could overcome her issues and support him.

Alone and on the brink of a new life that he didn't want, he was ready to end it all. It might have been the easy way out but he didn't have the strength needed to endure the future days. A lone ship lost in the middle of darkness, no one would mourn for him. He wouldn't be missed.

He closed his eyes and he could almost hear his drill instructor hollering at him. *Get up, Marine! There's no quit in a Marine.*

Staci Pence dropped her bag behind the nurses' desk and prepared to do her rounds on the ward to see who might be interested in talking with her. Twice a week she came to the hospital to meet with service members who needed someone to confide in, or just a friendly little chat. Sometimes it was easier to talk to someone who was there as a friend than it was to talk to a counselor.

She had seen the cost of war in her father's eyes. Now, in his memory, she did whatever she could to give back. One last semester and then she hoped to get a job at the hospital as a physical therapist. That would lead her to her ultimate dream of owning a horse ranch. She enjoyed being a physical therapist and maybe, somehow, she could still manage to do it, although the horse ranch was deeply engrained in her veins. *One step at a time and you'll reach your dreams.*

"Staci, I've got someone I'd like you to visit." Brenda moseyed up next to her and leaned against the counter.

"Anything you need." She looked down at the older woman, who was a good five inches shorter than her five foot six. The nurse's dark hair mixed with gray pulled back in a bun gave her a grandmotherly feel. Maybe that was why, over the past year during which Staci had been visiting the hospital patients, Brenda had taken her under her wing, leading her to the ones that needed someone the most, so she trusted Brenda's choice. "You going to give me the story on this patient or are you sending me in blind?"

"Private First Class Phillips is having a hard time adjusting to his life now."

A buzz from one of the machines in the room across the hall had Brenda moving away from the counter. "He's the last room on the right, but don't be surprised if he's unwilling to talk to you. He's a grumpy cat."

"I'll see what I can do for him." She tucked a strand of hair behind her ear and headed toward the room Brenda pointed out. She tried not to remember how many times her mother had said those very words. *Dad's having a hard time adjusting to life. Don't worry and go play.* Maybe if she had worried, or if PTSD wasn't something to be ashamed of, things would have been different. Back then, PTSD wasn't something that was talked about; it was a deep dark secret kept hidden away in shame. Everyone tried to forget it.

From the doorway, she could only make out a figure in bed. With the curtains drawn and the only light shining coming from the hallway, it was hard to make out any details. She tapped on the door. "Private First Class Phillips?"

"Go away," he ordered without looking toward the door.

"I'm not a doctor, I have no medication, and I'm not here to question you or give you orders."

"Then what do you want?"

She took that as close to an invite as she was going to get and strolled toward the bed. "Just to talk. We can discuss whatever you want. I'm only here to visit."

"Unless you brought whiskey, I don't want a visitor and I don't need anyone's pity. I just want to be left alone."

"Do whiskey brown eyes count?" As she neared the bed, she realized the sheets fell flat where his left leg should have been.

That time he did turn and glare at her, but after a moment, a small smile spread across his face. "While I might be able to get lost in those eyes, I was talking about a bottle of whiskey. Now you didn't just stumble upon my room, so who sent you?"

"One of the nurses, Brenda, thought you could use someone to talk to.

Someone that isn't here to judge you or determine if you're fit for duty. Just a friend." She raised an eyebrow at the deep laugh that vibrated his whole body.

"Fit for duty…" His words trailed off as he tugged back the sheet so she could see the full extent of his injuries. "You must be crazy. I'm being medically discharged. Everything I've worked for tossed down the drain. I should have died."

"You were given a second chance at life, which means you're meant to do something amazing."

"Like this? What good is half a man?"

She pulled the cover back over him, not because she was disgusted by what she saw but to keep the burns and bandages protected. "You're still the man you were before. Just because you're injured doesn't make you less so. Physical therapy will help you learn to use the prosthetic leg. You'll be able to walk and drive again. You can do the same with the prosthetic arm, but most get to the point where they become comfortable without it."

"How do you know so much about this? From what I can see, you have all your limbs intact."

"I'm in my last semester to become a physical therapist. I've worked with many amputees over the years, some through rehab but most of them right here in this hospital. I'm not going to lie to you and tell you it's easy but you're a Marine, you don't give up. You'll push through in the end. You'll be stronger and you'll get your life back."

"That's easy for you to say; you're not the cripple."

"I think you need to consider the fact things could be worse. You still have one good arm and leg. Some who come back don't have that. You'll learn to do things with your other arm and you will move past this. You survived. So many others didn't." She tried not to sound harsh but she knew first-hand the cost of war. His reactions were natural but from the look of things and the fact he wasn't drugged up from the pain, it was obvious he'd been there for some time.

He needed a wakeup call because, with his burns healing, he'd be discharged from the hospital in a few days.

"I'd rather have been one of those who didn't make it back. I'd have changed places with Weber in a heartbeat if it meant he'd be able to come back to his wife and son."

"You believe you're half a man because of your injuries, but you'd want someone else to suffer them instead of you. Cruel, isn't that?"

"If it meant he'd be here with his family, then yes, I'd gladly change places with him. Half a man is better than dead."

"You're right there, and you should be thankful you're still alive." She stood, grabbed one of the small cards she carried, and held it out to him. "My name and number. If you want to talk, call me and I'll stop by." When he didn't take it, she placed it on the bedside table.

"I don't need your pity."

"Good because I don't pity you." When she reached the door she turned back to look at him one final time. "Think about what I said. You've been given a second chance at life. Don't waste it."

She forced herself to walk from his room and into the hallway. To see him with such sadness in his eyes tore at her heart. That look was the same one her father had when he returned to the ranch. Only her father hadn't lost any limbs; he'd had burns over half his body from an incident that had killed the rest of this team. She might have been harsh on Phillips, but if it kept him from doing what her father did, then that's all that mattered. He needed to accept things as they were so he could move on and begin to live again.

"Any luck with PFC Phillips?" Brenda stood just a few feet away making notes in a chart.

"Not really. He's angry, and like you said, he's having a hard time dealing with this. Has a therapist spoken with him? Someone with more training than I have?"

"He has more than enough medical staff pestering him. What he needs is a friend. The only one that's come to visit him is Gunnery Sergeant Diamond, his old platoon sergeant. Even then, he barely acknowledged him."

"I'm not feeling very well today, but I'll come back in a few days and try to talk to him again."

"You're not coming down with something, are you?"

"No, nothing like that. Just a headache. My neighbor had a big bash yesterday and it ran late into the night. So with the lack of sleep and everything, it's not helping. I think I better head home." She continued on her way down the hall before Brenda could question her further. It wasn't a complete lie; she did have a minor headache, but it was due more to the memories that refused to leave her alone than to her neighbor's party.

She grabbed her bag from the nurses' station and sped up her pace. For the first time since she'd started coming to the hospital, she was in a rush to leave. She needed to put some distance between her and the PFC. What she didn't understand was why the memories came flooding back to her now. It had been years ago when her father was in a similar position to PFC Phillips and even then, she'd been just a little girl. What did she know about what her father had actually gone through? All she had to give her any insight about him was an old leather-bound journal he had kept a daily log in.

The journal had been mostly filled with rants, but it was the emotions within the words that got her. So full of hate, passion, anger, and love. The words that filled the pages showed the battle her father had gone through. No one had tried to help him. Maybe she was just one person but she tried to do her best to save just one life—so she did what she set out to do. She used her own tragedy to do something good and stop another family from suffering further loss. If more people helped then maybe the veterans' suicide rate wouldn't be so high.

Dad, I'm sorry no one saved you, but I'm doing my part to save my generation.

Chapter Two

Two days had passed since whiskey girl came to visit and Kyle couldn't get her off his mind. Her sweet country girl accent played through his thoughts. She was the first one who hadn't tried to pussyfoot around. The heat and sadness in her eyes made it almost seem liked she cared, but why would she? She didn't even know him. His gaze fell to the card still sitting on the bedside table. He hadn't moved it because he wasn't sure what he wanted to do with it yet. He wasn't going to call her but it didn't seem right to pitch it, either.

With his burns healing and the infection under control, he'd be discharged the following day. Then he'd never see her again. That very idea sent a twinge of sadness through him. "Get a hold of yourself. What would she want with you? She was only here to show sympathy and support, not because she actually cared."

Why would anyone care when his girlfriend hadn't even bothered to come see him in person to break things off? After a little more than a year dating, he'd learned her true nature. One he should have seen before but chose to remain in denial of his suspicions. He'd cared for her and hadn't wanted to see that side of her. She was a flag chaser—a woman only with a service member because of the uniform—and now he had nothing to offer her. She'd gone on to her next target and he was alone.

While he should have been grateful that she had just left him be instead of stringing him along even further, he couldn't help but see her betrayal as yet another loss. *Another thing this war has taken from me.* He'd joined the Marines to make a better life for himself. It wasn't like he had anything else. As a ward of the state, he had been tossed to the curb at eighteen with little money in his pocket and nowhere to go. The Marines were his way out. A way to make a life for himself. Even now, he wasn't sure what he was going to do. He had lived in the barracks on base so he had no apartment to go to when he was discharged the following day. Instead, he would be transported to a hotel, where he'd stay for a few days. Then, he'd either transfer into the wounded warrior housing facility when a space freed up or he could find something on his own and put a request in for off base housing. For now, anything would be better than looking at these pale gray walls and the awful stench of illness and bleach that seemed to cling to the place.

They had pushed for a medical halfway home to help him, but he had refused. He had been fitted for his prosthesis, and physical therapy to learn to walk on it would begin soon. In the meantime, he was stuck in the wheelchair.

Nothing screams cripple like a fucking wheelchair.

At least, he'd be out of this place and he could get some whiskey. His mouth watered at the very thought of that earthy flavor, so full bodied that it burned its way to the gut.

"Knock, knock." The woman from the other day stood in the doorframe. Her blonde hair, full of golden highlights, looked windblown while at the same time making her more attractive. The jeans and light brown sweater gave her an innocent look. She couldn't have been more than twenty-one.

"You again?" The emotions that swirled within him were too numerous to count. He didn't want to see her but a small part of him was intrigued by her. What brought her to this hospital? She didn't work on base, wasn't military; she was just a volunteer. What did she know about the struggles the patients here were dealing with? Sure, she was nearly finished with her degree in physical therapy, but she could work with anyone. Why amputees?

"Mind if I come in?"

"Suit yourself." He fiddled with the edge of the sheet as she strolled toward him. She grabbed the only chair in the room and came to sit next to him.

"I hear you're being discharged tomorrow. I'll bet you're glad to leave this place." She crossed a leg over the others and he couldn't tear his gaze from it as she did.

"I'm going from one prison to another. I'll spend the next several days at a hotel until I find somewhere else and get my request for off base housing approved. Somewhere wheelchair accessible until I've learned to walk with my prosthesis. At least I'll be able to have some privacy instead of staff popping in every two minutes."

"There are always benefits to every situation if you only look." She tipped her head to the card that still sat on the bedside table. "I see you still have that. Please, take it with you and call me if you want to talk."

"There are others here that need your help. Why take pity on a lost cause?"

"You're not a lost cause. Actually, I think you have a lot of potential if you can get through this, and if you let me and the others help, you will." They sat there in silence for a long moment before she leaned forward. "So, Private First Class Phillips, tell me about yourself."

Private First Class. Would there ever come a time those words wouldn't send shooting pains through his chest and ice his veins? One damn moment changed everything.

"Private…"

"Kyle!" His voice rose but he couldn't help it. "Please, Kyle, just Kyle." He said it over and over again as if he could forget his title as a Marine and just be Kyle. To rewind to a few years earlier when he was but a kid, living life to the fullest—to just before he'd gone to the recruiter. Then, none of this would have happened.

"Okay, Kyle." She placed a hand on the bed, but didn't touch him. "Are you okay?"

"Fine." He took a deep breath and forced the memories away. "What do you want to know?"

"One of the nurses said you haven't had any visitors since you've been here, except your Gunnery Sergeant. Where's your family?"

"You go for the heart of things, don't you?" Not that he had any doubt about that. She had already proved she was feisty. "If we're going to do this, then we play by my rules. For every question you ask, you have to answer one about yourself. Deal?"

She paused and seemed to be considering it for a moment before she finally nodded. "This isn't how it normally works, but okay. My question still stands."

"I was a ward of the state until I turned eighteen. No parents or siblings. Even my best friend is…dead." He swallowed the lump in his throat at the very thought of Weber. "What about your family?"

"My mother's still in Kentucky where she's a veterinarian. She's unhappy that I'm not following in her footsteps. No siblings."

"What about your father?"

She raised an eyebrow at him. "I thought this was one question each. I'll answer it but it will cost you two. My father died years ago. Now, your turn. Why did you join the Marines?"

He pressed the button to raise the bed a little. No matter how much he tried, he couldn't get away from that topic. Just as the foster care was a part of his life, so were the Marines, and neither topic was one he wanted to discuss. "I aged out of the system and needed something. Joining the military seemed to be the best idea because it gave me everything I needed. As for the Marines, that just kind of happened. I went to the recruiting office and a Marine spoke to me. I signed up and shipped off to boot camp a week later."

"Since you just fell into the military, what did you grow up wanting to do?"

"Crazy as it sounds, I wanted to be an accountant. Something about numbers always drew me in. Math was the one class in school I excelled at. Everything else I goofed off and hated every moment of it." He thought back to his high school math teacher, who'd inspired him to do better. She told him he could do whatever he wanted if he only applied himself. "Why physical therapy?"

"It's a means to an end."

"Huh?" He wasn't sure what she meant.

"It's kind of a long story." She adjusted and scooted her chair closer to the bed. "When I was young I wanted to be a doctor. I wanted to help people, but I was raised on a horse ranch and I've always wanted to own one. There's a certain one I've had my eye on for years. When I sat down and really thought about it, I realized that dream was more important to me than being a doctor. This will get me there."

"A ranch—interesting. What made it more important?" He realized he'd asked a second question before she got to slip in hers.

"My father was a horse trainer and always wanted to own one but life had other plans. So I'm going to do it in his memory. But now, I get two questions. Why have you turned away those who have tried to help you?"

"Prying." He tugged the blankets up farther, trying to ease his discomfort. "I don't need help."

"Liar."

"That's not a question," he pointed out.

"You haven't answered my question honestly, so it still stands." She uncrossed her legs and leaned closer. "You've been through a lot. There's so much pain in your eyes but you refuse to talk to anyone. Why?"

"What I've seen isn't any worse than what others have witnessed or lived through. All they want to do is give me drugs. I don't want drugs that will make me forget, cloud my judgement, or act like a zombie. I'm learning to live with my ghosts."

"You don't want prescription drugs; instead you'd prefer whiskey. Alcohol will only help you forget for a little while. You'll need to talk about it to move forward."

"What do you know about it?"

"More than you think." She stood and moved away from the bed. "My father...his Army service changed him. Not just physically with his burns, but also mentally. He came home to us different. At first, he chose alcohol as a way to keep the memories at bay, but as the weeks passed he had to drink more and more to do the job. Eventually, it wasn't enough and he took other means to end the horrible thoughts...permanently."

"I'm sorry for your loss, but things are different for me."

"Isn't that what everyone thinks?"

She kept her back to him and, had it been months ago, before he'd ended up as a cripple, he'd have gone to her. Comforted her. Instead, he lay in that bed, useless, and it confirmed once again that he'd never be good enough. *Stop taking up space and resources that could help someone else. You're not worth it any longer.*

"I lost my father because no one helped him. Maybe he was like you and wouldn't let anyone in but Mom tried to shelter me from his *problems.* The only time I had any quality time with Dad was when she was on a vet call and we were on the ranch together, taking care of the horses. We bonded over that but I could tell something was wrong. It wasn't until my senior year in high school that I found his journals."

"Journals." It might have been sexist but he had always thought that was more of a woman thing.

"Yeah." She turned to glance at him. "Don't sound so surprised; a lot of men keep journals. It's also not uncommon for those in counseling to do it. Dad never went to see a counselor so I'm not sure why he started writing one.

Maybe it was because he did it with the horses. He kept a journal of their lives for the owners. Accomplishments, training, everything. He might have thought getting it down on paper would help. I'm not sure, but it left me with an insight about him that I never had before."

"So that's why you're here? You couldn't save your father, so now I'm what? A surrogate?"

She spun around on her heels to face him, her face alight with anger as she glared at him. "How dare you?"

"Hit a sore spot?" The pain in her eyes almost stopped him—she didn't deserve him lashing out at her—but the need to keep her off him proved too overpowering. "Well, I don't like being a replacement for someone you couldn't save. I've said it a thousand times before and I'll say it again: I'm fine. I don't need anyone's help, pity, or anything else."

"Fine. I know there's plenty of others here who would love the company." She nearly ran to the door, but paused before she passed through. "I wish you all the best. Don't let the people that care about you down because you don't like me. You can get through this." With that, she was gone.

Don't let people down…if only I hadn't already. If only I hadn't changed places with you, Weber, you'd still be alive. Crippled but alive to be with your wife and child.

Staci spent the next two hours visiting with those who actually wanted her company. Yet, even as she tried to make small talk with the ones she had come to know, her thoughts continued to wander back to PFC Phillips. He'd tried to hide it but the pain he felt inside dug deeper than she had imagined. No one could help him until he was ready, but even with that knowledge, she couldn't just sit on the sidelines and wait. Tomorrow, when he was discharged, he'd turn to the one thing her father had sought comfort from as well—alcohol. Even if he found solace in it, this would only be temporary. What the bottle led to would be worse, possibly even fatal. That wasn't something she could live with.

She wanted to wander back down the hall to his room to get him to see reason. It wouldn't be as easy as that. She could try as much as she wanted but until he could see what he was doing to himself and became aware he did still have a future, she might as well try to help a solid brick wall fall down with her bare hands.

You're only doing this because you couldn't save your father…

Maybe he was right. She had started to volunteer with service members because of the impact of her father's return from war and his suicide had on her life, but it wasn't what kept her going day after day. She continued to volunteer because of what she saw. She watched as those who'd seen unimaginable horrors came to terms with their grief and made their lives better. They didn't let the horrors they'd witnessed keep them down. Rather, they lived for the ones who would never make it back home to their families. They took joy from the little things. They'd watch the sunrise as if they'd never seen it before.

That's why she did what she did.

It didn't matter if someone was for or against the war. What mattered was, America was there for those who put everything on the line to stand up and fight for freedom. America is what it is because of those who are willing to fight for the land and the people's rights. She was only doing a small part to give back. *I'm not giving up on you, PFC Phillips. You're worth fighting for.*

Chapter Three

Days had passed with Kyle only seeing the four walls of his hotel room and it was beginning to make him stir-crazy. He needed to get out, but his fear of facing the rest of the world in his condition kept him in his room. He saw how people at the hotel had looked at him, how the pizza delivery guy's mouth dropped open a little when Kyle opened the door. People were shocked at his appearance and there was nothing he could do to change it. The prosthesis wouldn't change that. The burns would still be there, taunting him. Every time he looked in the mirror and every phantom pain from where his limbs should have been were constant reminders.

He berated himself for not having the courage to just end it. To eliminate the pain he felt and the horror he saw in others' eyes. He had his sidearm in the nightstand drawer, but all he could do was open that drawer and stare at it. Every time he thought he could go ahead and do the deed, his courage fled. He didn't understand the reason. He had no more purpose, and nothing and no one in his life any longer. So why delay the inevitable?

He slid the drawer open again and the card from the woman at the hospital slid off the book next to his sidearm. *Staci Pence*. Her name stared up at him in a bold, fancy font that seemed to match her personality.

Call her. Before he could stop himself, he picked up his cell phone and called. It rang once, twice…by the third ring doubt crept in and he hit the end button. "What was I thinking?" He didn't need that woman, or her fiery spirit and pure soul, trying to make the world a better place. She didn't need to be tainted by him. Not when she could do so much for others.

His cell vibrated in his hand and he glanced down at it. The same number he had just called displayed on screen. He wanted to answer it, to hear her voice and the calming reassurance he knew he'd find in it, but he didn't dare give in to the temptation. He tossed the phone on the bed.

Pushing his wheelchair over to the window, he stared out. From the second floor window, he could watch as people went about their lives, and cars sped down the road in a hurry to get wherever they were going. If only people realized life was precious, that it shouldn't be rushed. That everyone should take the time to enjoy each day. A year ago he had been just like them, but not anymore. The military had started the change in him and his injuries had done the rest. Unlike everyone dashing from one place to another, he no longer had a life like that, and possibly one day it would be too late for one of the people he observed below to slow down and enjoy life as well.

You never know what you have until it's gone. The words of one of the mothers in a foster home he had spent time in played in his thoughts. Only, when she'd said them, she was referring to the fact he had just been kicked out of another home for acting up. Foster home after foster home and not one of them had ever made him feel like he belonged. Being tossed around from one home to another hadn't worked. It came to a point where he had to just suck it up and wait until he aged out of the system.

Suck it up and wait… He wasn't sure that would work now. What was he waiting for? Death?

Twice, Staci called the number and both times, she got voicemail. *Kyle Phillips*

here and you know what to do. She didn't bother to leave a message. He had called but hung up before she could answer and now he wasn't picking up. What if something happened? He could have decided to end things like her father. It would be all her fault she hadn't saved him because she hadn't answered.

"Are you coming?" her friend called from the table. "The hand's dealt; we're just waiting on you."

Tonight, was supposed to be an evening for just the two of them but Kate's boyfriend had the evening off so it had turned into a threesome. Staci felt like an extra wheel but after cancelling the last girls' night with Kate, she didn't feel right about bowing out again. Now, she had an excuse. *It's not an excuse, it's a good reason. Kyle needs me.*

"Kate, I'm sorry…"

"Don't tell me one of those *soldiers* need you." Kate let out a deep sigh and leaned back in her chair. "When are you going to stop going there? You have a life to lead with college, work, friends. It's all demanding; you don't need to waste your time there. They've got the help they need. What do they need you for?"

"You don't understand."

"You're right, I don't," Kate continued, her voice raised. "I don't understand why you'd rather hang out with someone who's messed up when you have us. It's not like you know any of them."

This was the only rift in their friendship and it was huge. Kate had never understood and never would. No matter how many times they had the conversation, Kate couldn't see Staci's side. To her, it was practically like visiting the grave of a loved one—another thing her friend didn't do. She couldn't see the reasoning behind visiting a gravestone of someone departed.

"Kate, you're my friend and I wish you'd supported my choices. Either way, this is something that is important to me and I'm going." She grabbed her bag from the side of the sofa. "I'm sorry, but I'm sure you can find other ways to enjoy your evening without me."

"She's right K, let her go." Kate's boyfriend slid his hand under her shirt.

At that moment, Staci couldn't think of the new boyfriend's name and didn't really care; she was only thankful for the diversion. He'd entertain Kate and Staci wouldn't feel so bad for bailing on her friend.

"Whatever. Just go." Kate's words hinted that the fight wasn't over.

Right now it didn't matter to her; she'd deal with it later. With one last glance at Kate and the boyfriend, Staci headed for the door. The two of them had been roommates before Kate had decided she could no longer stand the rift Staci's volunteer work had caused between them. She'd moved out to live with this newest boyfriend, leaving the small two bedroom house located between the hospital and the college all to Staci. Making ends meet might have been harder and limited what she could stash away for the ranch, but it had given her some privacy. She hadn't realized how nice it was to have a place all to herself and not have to deal with a roommate bringing people over at any given hour.

She slid behind the wheel and started her pickup truck when the realization dawned on her. She didn't know where he was. Was he still at the hotel or had he finally been transferred to one of the wounded warrior units? Not knowing where else to go, she headed for the hotel at which most of those who were discharged from the hospital without anywhere else to go ended up. If she failed to find him there, she wasn't sure where else to look.

Rush hour was over, so the traffic was light as she drove across town. She pulled into a parking spot close to the door and checked the rearview mirror. Without having his room number, she'd have to make nice with whoever was on duty at the front desk. If she was having a lucky night, it would be one of the regulars who knew her from when she came to visit the others who had stayed here. If she wasn't, then she might have made this trip for nothing. She might have anyways, because she wasn't even sure he was staying here. He could have been at one of the other hotels, or maybe he had found his own place. It had been a week since she had last seen him so anything was possible.

"Here goes nothing." She hopped out of her truck and headed for the main entrance.

The cool breeze chilled her and helped to ease her nerves. She was scared of what she might find in Kyle's room. He might need more help than she could give. She wasn't a therapist and had never tried to be one. She only wanted to lend a supporting shoulder and be someone they could confide in if needed.

"Hey there, Staci." The young check-in clerk stood behind the counter. The black sleek finish of the wood made the silver hotel emblem before it stand out in sharp contrast. "What brings you here?"

"Hi." She strolled across the lobby, her heels clicking off the titled floor as she made her way toward him. She waited until one of the guests, who had followed her in, moved to the elevator before she revealed her reason for being there. "I've stopped by to visit a friend from the hospital, Kyle Phillips, but I forgot to check his room number before I left."

"He's here." He shook his hair that came to the tops of his ears away from his eyes and looked at her. "Haven't seen him around though. He doesn't leave his room."

"I know, that's why I'm here."

"Things bad with him?" He leaned forward, intrigued by what she might tell him.

"You know I can't tell you what's up with him," she told him lightly without being rude because she needed his help. He didn't have to tell her what room he was in. "I can tell you that I'm hoping I can help him and maybe you'll see more of him. So, where can I find him?"

"You know this could cost me my job." Even as he spoke, he clicked a few buttons on the keyboard. "Room two hundred and thirty-nine. Second floor, end of the hall."

"I owe you." She gave him her biggest smile and headed for the elevators.

"Bring me some of those delicious chocolate chip cookies of yours and we'll call it even."

"This weekend." The elevator doors slid open; she stepped inside and pushed the second floor button. The doors closed, and she had a moment to think before she arrived at the second floor. In the week he had been there, no one had seen much of him. It didn't surprise her, but it wasn't a good sign. Had he kept his appointments at the hospital? Had he continued his therapy with his prosthesis?

She stood in front of the door to his room, took a deep breath, and knocked. This was what she'd come for and it was the only way to get the answers to her questions.

"Who is it?"

"Staci...you called me." Silence met her words. "Come on Kyle, open up. I'm not going anywhere. Even if I have to stay out here all night."

The door flung open and there before her he sat in the wheelchair, dark circles under his eyes. "I didn't invite you here. How did you get my room number?"

"I've got ways. Now are you going to invite me in or shall we discuss things in the hallway?" He rolled his chair back, giving her enough room to step inside. "Thank you."

"I'd rather be alone."

"I've no doubt about that." She glanced around the room. The only light came through the open curtains. The bed looked slightly rumpled as if he had tried to sleep not long before she arrived, but other than that, the room was spotless. She wasn't sure if that was one of the benefits of living in a hotel with room service or if it was Kyle's doing. "When you didn't answer I became worried."

"Calling you was a mistake." He shut the door and rolled toward the window.

Or maybe it was your cry for help. She didn't say this aloud because that would only make him angry. "All you had to do was answer and let me know, then I wouldn't have shown up."

"How was I supposed to know you'd come here?" he snapped with his gaze averted. "Now that you know, you can leave."

"Kyle…" She stepped toward him. "You called me because things got too rough and you wanted to talk to someone. I'm here now; don't push me away."

"I don't need anyone. I've done fine on my own all these years."

"There's no reason to go through life alone when you've got someone who's willing to stand by your side." She came to kneel next to him. "I'm here, let me help you."

How could she get through to him? If there existed a magical saying that would help her, she wasn't aware of it. In the time she'd spent working with veterans, she'd never had someone affect her as Kyle did. Most of the time, either they wanted her company or they didn't. If they didn't, she'd respect it.

Kyle was different because Brenda had asked her to help him as a special case. He didn't have family, which left him alone at the mercy of medical professionals. Sometimes, they weren't the easiest to confide in. Usually, veterans had someone to turn to—loved ones who'd bend over backwards to see these wounded warriors overcome their impossible challenges.

Kyle had no one. *No one.*

Her dad had her mother, but she'd been isolated from his pain. Sometimes, you can be around people yet still feel alone. She never stopped wondering *what if…?* Kyle had a death wish, and if she didn't step in to help, he may go ahead and fulfil it.

There was also something else about him. Something she couldn't deny. *Something* that didn't just stir the heartstrings but also the woman within. Hints of the man he's been before his injuries shined through occasionally and made her want to dig through the outer shell until she found that man again.

Chapter Four

Even as Kyle tried to push Staci away, he wanted her to stay. He missed being around people, and she made him feel like a normal man. She didn't treat him like a cripple or look at him like so many others had. There were no questions about what had happened to cause his injuries. She just seemed to accept things as they were—maybe because of everything she had seen working at the hospital, or her experience training as a physical therapist, but either way it put him at an ease he hadn't felt in a long time.

At first, they made small talk, and then they just sat there by the window. The silence wasn't uncomfortable, it felt much like they had known each other long enough to be relaxed together. The last rays of sun disappeared and the sky darkened. Night descended upon them. This was the time he hated the most; he felt more vulnerable in the dark and his ghosts wouldn't let him free.

"You know, when I was young, I always thought there were monsters lurking within the dark."

"I think all kids do." She tipped her head to the side to look at him. "I was terrified that something was living under my bed. Every night my father would come in and *cleanse* my room of evil. None of us realize we have no idea what evil truly is until it bites us in the ass."

"I couldn't have said it better myself." He turned and met her gaze. "Only the evil isn't under our beds or in our closets. It's waiting for us out there. For some it's a robbery gone wrong or a car accident. For me, it happened overseas. A fucking IED stole the life I was meant to have and for what? What did Weber's sacrifice get us?"

"Things don't always turn out how we want them to and I'm sorry for what happened. It was awful and nothing I can say will make that better, but if you focus on the positives, it will help you get through each day. I'm not going to tell you one day you won't remember this because you always will. Things will get easier but it will never go away completely. I told you before that if you talk about it—"

"I don't know how to talk about it." He paused and let out a deep sigh. "How do you talk about the fact you're responsible for your best friend's death?"

"Weber?"

He nodded. "I thought I was saving him by changing places with him, but it ultimately caused his death. If I'd have left him where he was, he'd still be here…"

"And you'd be dead," she supplied.

"Yes, dead, but Weber would be here with his wife, Cassy, and his son. Crippled but alive."

"Stop that." She leaned forward. "Stop calling yourself a cripple. You're alive, and yes, you've lost two of your limbs, but that doesn't make you less human."

He let out a light chuckle. He *was* a lot less; he couldn't do most things he had once been able to do. "The point is, he'd have a reason to fight through this shit."

She stared at him for a moment before her eyebrow arched in question. "You haven't been to physical therapy, have you?"

"What's the point?"

"The point is learning to walk with your prosthesis. Learning to use your prosthetic arm. You'll be able to get your life back and do whatever you want. You won't be stuck in a wheelchair any longer and can move around as you wish. Isn't that what you want?"

"What I want…" He dragged his hand over his face, the ruff stubble along his cheek rubbed against his palm. "Screw it, it doesn't matter."

"Go on. It matters to me."

"I want the life I had back."

She reached forward and laid her hand on his forearm. "Then let me help you. You don't have to do this alone, I'll help in any way I can, but it starts with you going to PT."

"You never give up, do you?" When she shook her head, he added, "You're going to be an amazing physical therapist. No one will be able to slack off when you're around."

"That's the goal." She smirked. "Seriously though, let me help you."

"I'm a bigger project than you want to take on." He brushed her offer to the side and tried to think about anything besides her touch. She was the first person that wasn't a doctor or nurse to touch him. He hadn't realized how much he missed the simplest touches of a friend or lover until she laid her hand on his. "Do you know why I called tonight?"

"Partially, yes." She didn't move her hand away from his arm; instead, she let her fingers tease along curve of it. "You were finally reaching out for help. That's a huge step."

"It was selfish." He closed his eyes. "With thoughts of ending it all, I pulled open the drawer where I keep my sidearm, and your card fell down to land on top. Your name and number jumped at me for the first time, like it was meant to be. I called before I could stop myself, but when it rang my courage fled and I hung up. I didn't expect you to come here, but that brief call, even though I hadn't spoken to you, had given me the little bit of strength I needed to carry on."

"That weakness and doubt will come again. Next time, will you have the will power to call me or will your courage flee then, too? Kyle…" She paused a moment and waited for him to look at her. "I don't want to see something happen to you."

"Is this because of your father again?"

She gave his arm a light squeeze. "No, it's because of you. I want to help you. If you won't go back to the hospital then we'll figure out something."

"I'm not going to the hospital. I can't do that again. I just need…time." He wasn't sure what he needed but time sounded reasonable.

"Fine, we'll get through it another way." She took her hand away and leaned back. Her brows arched together in thought.

Without her hand on his arm, sadness and longing tugged at him. He reminded himself again that she could never be interested in him in any way besides friendship. No women ever would be, not with his condition. A nasty pill to swallow, but to him, that was the truth. His ex-girlfriend had proved that.

"You'll come to my place."

"What?" Her statement pulled him from his thoughts, leaving him feeling like he had missed something.

"I've got a two bedroom ranch house I'm renting not far from the hospital. There are no steps and the hallways are big enough that your wheelchair will fit. It's not much, but it's in a quiet little area. My former roommate moved in with her boyfriend so I have a spare room. You'll come stay with me."

"You can't be serious?"

"I am. It's the perfect solution. You need somewhere to stay and not live in this hotel room. I'll be close by so you'll have the support you need without being in the hospital. However, there are two conditions."

He couldn't believe the woman before him. She was seriously inviting a strange man to move in with her. "What would your father say if he knew you were inviting strangers to come live with you?"

"I know you better than I knew Kate when she moved in with me. Same thing about anyone else who could move in as a roommate. So why would he have a problem with it? My mother, on the other hand, would have a fit but she has one over just about everything I do. She wanted me to become a vet like her. When I told her what I wanted to do she couldn't believe it. She hates the idea of me buying the ranch someday." She tucked a strand of hair behind her ear. "That's not the point. I'm an adult, and who I choose to have in my home is my business."

That was the feisty side of her that he was beginning to like. "I don't think it's a good idea, but what are your two conditions?"

"The first is easy: you must hand over your sidearm. I've got a small safe in my room that we'll put it in. It's for your protection. I don't want those thoughts you had before to return and you act on them. Suicide is not the answer. We'll get through this, *together*."

"Taking a Marine's sidearm is like taking his arm." The words came out before he had time to think about what he was saying; as they sank in, he looked down at his body and chuckled. "I guess since I've lost an arm already, it's nothing."

"Do you realize what just happened?" She didn't give him time to answer. "You forgot, even if only for a nanosecond, that you lost your arm. You were even able to make a smart remark about it once you remembered. That's an improvement over referring to yourself as a cripple."

"If you can't laugh at yourself, who can? Plus, I think I've got enough material for a standup comedy act. Now what's your second condition?" The first one wasn't too bad and he might actually consider it, even just to get out of this hotel room with the pale white walls and hard-as-a-rock bed. He had slept in softer ditches than that bed.

"You must go to PT. I can help you at home with your prosthesis but I don't have the equipment that is needed to get you started. You'll start out learning to stand on it using the parallel bars. That's the first step. I know you've been fitted for it but haven't actually participated in any therapy using it."

"I cancelled this week's appointments." He admitted. "I just didn't feel like it was worth wasting their time if I was only going to…" He trailed off before mentioning suicide again.

"Well, not anymore. You'll go, and we'll have you walking again in no time."

"Besides the bars, what should I expect?" He hated the unease and nervousness in his voice. Fear of the unknown had been one of the reasons he had cancelled the PT appointments.

"Every physical therapist is different regarding how they want you to start. For me, I normally start with the parallel bars. They are designed to help you get used to putting weight on your prosthesis and they can make a person more comfortable with their new limb. With your partial loss of arm on that side as well, I'd raise the bars so that at first you'll be supporting yourself by your armpits, sort of like crutches, and have you get used to it. This way you wouldn't have all your weight on one side."

"Sounds like a bitch." Though it was a lot less complicated than his mind had created. He had expected to be stuck in the wheelchair for months while he learned to get around on the prosthesis.

"It's not that bad and the important thing is, you'll be walking again in no time. After you get used to having weight on the prosthesis, you'll progress to slow walking, using the bars for support. When you're ready, you'll practice walking. Some choose to use the aid of a cane at first while others don't need it." They sat there in silence for a moment before she added, "I don't know the details of your situation but a below the knee amputation that is healing well could allow for you to be up and walking in a week. Everyone is different but it all depends on your strength and how much you want it."

"Trust me. I want out of this chair bad." Even as he said this, he knew it was true. Crazy that he had cancelled the appointments when he wanted to be able to move about again with the ease of two legs. *Even if one is fake.*

"That will help. Your burns are mostly healed now, but because of them you were stuck in the hospital longer. Otherwise, you'd have already been up walking around." She smiled at him. "See, you were worried for nothing. So will you keep your next appointment?"

"I will." His moods were like a pendulum, swinging back and forth. Except for him, it was from high to low and the lows seemed to last longer than the highs. An hour before he had wanted to kill himself; now he was making plans for Monday and it was only Saturday.

"So what do you say about coming home with me?"

"I say you're nuts." He chuckled. "You have no idea what you're inviting into your home."

"I know you're capable of a lot of things, but I don't think you'll hurt me."

"Not intentionally." He couldn't keep the sadness out of his voice, but what scared him the most about staying at her place was the fact she could get hurt because of him. If she came to him in the midst of one of his dreams, he could lash out without realizing until it was too late.

"Are you having nightmares? Flashbacks?" Her back stiffened as if she was suddenly uncomfortable.

"Rethinking your offer?" He teased.

"No, the offer stands, as does the question."

"Nightmares come and go. So if I'm going to come then we need to set up boundaries." He ran his hand down the arm of the chair and refused to look at her. "If you hear me…dreaming…you stay the hell away from me. I won't have you getting hurt because I didn't know it was you."

"Don't worry, I know all too well." Before he could ask, she explained, "Dad had only been back on the ranch a few days when one of our mares was giving birth. It was dark but I had snuck out to check on her, because I knew she was due any day. When I got to the barn, I found out something was wrong. I learned later that what I had heard wasn't just from her giving birth. I rushed into the house and to Dad's bedroom. He freaked out when I woke him." Her shoulders slumped and leaned back against the chair, almost as if deflated.

"Are you okay?"

"I just realized that was the start of the breakdown. It was the first of the tumbling blocks that came falling down. Less than a month later he was dead."

Before he could stop himself, he scooted his chair closer to her and took her hand in his. "I'm truly sorry for your loss, but you have to know that what happened wasn't your fault."

"I know it." The tears in her eyes glistened as she tried to give him a smile that fell flat. "I do, but sometimes it's hard to remember that. If only someone had been there to help him. If PTSD hadn't been treated like some dark secret, maybe he'd still be alive."

"The war in Iraq and Afghanistan has brought attention to PTSD like never before but a person still needs to seek the help. It's like an alcoholic. The people around him can try to get him to stop drinking but until he's ready it won't help. They have to hit rock bottom in order to accept what is being offered."

"You speak as if from experience."

He was but he didn't know where to start to explain it to her. Would he talk about his parents first? Or himself, his own life? Could he speak of one without the other? He decided he didn't want to go down the path to the past. "When I was at the hospital I wanted nothing to do with any of it but being here, cooped up in this hotel room, something changed. For the last week I've sat by this window watching the people go about their lives and I've missed that feeling of being one of them—among them. I've never been the life of the party, or even someone who enjoyed being around crowds, but I've never been so lonely in all my life."

"We can change that." She placed her other hand on top of his. "You're not alone, and I'll help in any way I can."

Chapter Five

Staci wasn't sure what had possessed her to invite him to come stay with her, but the offer stood. She wanted to help him, but she also wanted to get to know him better. Something about him intrigued her and she wanted to explore it. The hours passed as they sat there in his hotel room just talking. Nothing as deep as their previous conversations, but just getting to know each other as two people instead of as a wounded Marine and a volunteer college student. They bonded over tales of their childhood, their hopes and dreams.

Sometime during their conversations, he had talked her into sitting on the bed because the only chair in the room was as hard as sitting on concrete. She leaned back on the bed and yawned. It had grown late but she wasn't leaving him unless he threw her out. Next time those thoughts came, he might not have the strength to shut the drawer on the gun and she wasn't about to lose him.

"You should go home and get some rest." He tried again.

"Not until you agree to come with me."

"I told you I want you to think about your offer before we make any agreements. That means you need to go home and sleep. Tomorrow..." He glanced at the clock and they both realized it was well after midnight. "Well, I guess later today, we'll discuss it again."

"Nothing's going to change so you might as well come with me. Otherwise you're stuck with me until the sun comes up." She was glad she didn't have any classes tomorrow so she could sleep during the day. Either way, she wasn't leaving him. He had admitted once it got dark it was harder to push the thoughts of suicide away.

"I'm not going to do anything stupid, so you can go home with a clear mind."

"Like I said, unless you're kicking me out, you're stuck with me." She forced her eyes open and considered getting up for another cup of coffee but that seemed like too much work.

"Then at least get some sleep. You're exhausted."

"I'm fine."

"Just close your eyes and sleep. Even if I wanted to, I wouldn't do anything. I wouldn't leave you to find my body when you woke. I'm…injured not stupid."

Knowing he had almost said crippled instead of injured, she raised an eyebrow at him. "Close call there."

"I'm learning." He smirked. "Now, who said you couldn't teach an old dog new tricks?"

She wanted to throw him a snippy comeback but her brain seemed to be on strike. "Sorry, I'm not the best company. Between my classes, work, and the hospital, most nights I fall into bed exhausted. But that's all about to change."

"Why's that?"

"When I first moved here to start college, I took a position at a doctor's office as an office assistant. Well, Friday was my last day working there. Starting Monday I'll work from home, doing the billing and bookkeeping. I'll have more work than I did in the office but I'll be able to work my own hours and at my own pace, no interruptions."

He eyed her for a moment. "How old are you?"

To get a better look at him, she turned onto her side and adjusted the pillow under her head. "Don't you know it's rude to ask a lady her age? Second, that question came out of the blue."

"Not completely out of the blue. You mentioned college and it got me thinking. You're about to finish your Masters in Physical Therapy, but you don't look old enough."

"Mom wasn't very pleased with the schools in our area so she homeschooled me. The benefit of that was I finished earlier than my peers. She also enrolled me in college classes when I was still in high school. So, when I actually started college I already had credits coming with me. After my first semester I realized things were slower than I was used to and doubled my class load. I've been able to complete my degrees in half the time. But, to answer your question, I just turned twenty last month."

"Before you ask, I'm twenty-one and as for your other question, foster care taught me to ask what I needed to know, otherwise I'd never find out."

"Huh?"

"As a foster child you're overlooked so if you have a question, you just ask it. I never worried about being rude because I was never there long enough. Tossed around like an unwanted dog for most of my life, I've never worried about upsetting people. The Marines were the first time I had any real structure."

"I'm sorry."

"Don't be." He shrugged as if it didn't matter, but there was a twinge of sadness to it. "Everyone has something they'd rather forget and that's mine."

"That explains why you didn't have family visiting…" She reached up and covered her mouth. "I shouldn't have said that. Lack of sleep is messing with my brain and I'm saying things before I think them through. It was rude and I apologize."

"It's the truth and there's no reason to be sorry. You're right, it's just me. The friends I've made in the military have even disappeared, but who can blame them. No one wants to face what might happen to them. We all know the possibilities but no one needs to see that horror before them. I'm alone."

"Not anymore."

"Everyone leaves eventually." He mumbled without meeting her gaze.

"Not everyone and not me." Her eyes fluttered shut and as much as she tried to pry them back open, they wouldn't cooperate.

A blanket was pulled over her, covering her in warmth. She wanted to thank him, but the words died on her tongue. Before sleep wrapped its arms around her and pulled her into its embrace, she realized one thing. Some time since she met Kyle, her desire changed from being there to help someone in memory of her father to wanting to be there for him. She was beginning to care about him, far more than she cared about anyone else before.

The night had passed without any issues and now the sun was beginning to peek over the horizon. Kyle spent the night trying to immerse himself in a book he had picked up, but all he could think about was the woman lying in his bed. She was beautiful, emitting a peaceful glow as she slept.

He needed to keep his thoughts about her in check. Letting his mind wonder what her lips tasted like, or how she would feel pressed against his body, would get him nowhere. She deserved better than him. She deserved a whole man, not someone that couldn't even hold her properly. A few months ago, he'd have made a move and she wouldn't have been sleeping alone now. But back then, he wouldn't have even known her—wouldn't have had a reason to. Life threw curve ball after curve ball at him and he had no choice but to roll with it.

A soft moan escaped her lips as she stretched and woke up. "You haven't been sitting there all night, have you?"

He sat the book aside. "Someone fell asleep in my bed."

"It's huge. You could have joined me."

"That wouldn't have been a very gentlemanly thing to do. I hope you slept well and now that you're up, I'll order breakfast from room service."

"Coffee's fine for me." She scooted up in the bed. "You really should have either woke me or come to bed. There was plenty of room. You need rest too if you're going to take on physical therapy this week."

"Nice reminder thrown in there, but don't worry, I haven't changed my mind."

"Then have you considered my other suggestion?"

"Moving in with you?" He wheeled over to the coffee pot and set it to brew. "I have and I've decided that if your offer still stands I will *rent* your second bedroom. I should have been looking for a place to stay since I left the hospital, but I haven't left this room. Today, that's going to change." It was going to change, but he wasn't sure for how long. His moods had been all over the place since he returned from overseas. One minute he was feeling completely hopeless wanting to end things and hours later, he was determined to make the most of his second chance at life. It was an endless battle but, at the moment, one he was determined to win.

"Very well, but my requirements still stand. I want your gun."

He nodded to the nightstand. "My sidearm is in there." Weapons became a part of him since he joined the Marines; they'd kept him safe, but he was willing to let her keep the gun for the time being. Not because he thought he'd actually use the weapon, but because having it out of his hands would make her feel safer. If he was going to kill himself, there were other ways.

"How did you get it anyways?"

"I purchased it and a bottle of whiskey the day I was discharged from the hospital. I had plans to use it that night, but as you can see, I didn't."

"Did the whiskey get you drunk and save your life?"

"No, the whiskey remained untouched." *It was those whiskey brown eyes of yours that saved me that night. I couldn't get them out of my thoughts. The sadness that showed in them as if you were already disappointed in me.*

She pulled out the nightstand drawer and reached for the holstered gun. "What's this?" She held up his new rank insignia with the chevron and the two crossed rifles below it.

The morning he had been discharged from the hospital, he had been promoted to Lance Corporal. He had shoved the insignia away in the drawer and tried to forget about it. He didn't feel like he deserved the position and the haunting memory that Weber should have been promoted then as well only made things that much harder to accept.

"You've been promoted? You're a…" She looked down at the badge again. "Sorry, I'm not sure what comes after PFC. A Sergeant?"

"Lance Corporal," he supplied. "It was in the works before my injuries, but came through the morning I left the hospital."

"Congratulations."

"Joy. Maybe we should crack open that bottle of whiskey and celebrate." He tipped his head toward the drawer where the alcohol was also stashed. Everything close at hand so that, if he ever gave up, he could find comfort with them.

"I think not." She took the weapon and the whiskey and shoved them into the bag she'd tossed on the bed. "But we can celebrate in another way. We'll pack your stuff up and head over to my place. I'll shower, and then make us a delicious meal. No room service or takeaway. Then we'll spend the day watching movies and eating popcorn, because tomorrow I'm dropping you off at the hospital and we're going to get you back on your feet."

"Foot." He smirked, unable to believe he was joking about his condition.

"Feet, foot, what does it matter? What matters is you'll be walking again. Then driving, and everyone should watch out for that." She smirked.

For some reason, he had a feeling this was the beginning of his new life. The time had come for him to start working to better himself because, if he was going to live, this wasn't the way to do it. He needed to be able to walk, drive, and do everything that he could do before. He had to pull himself up by his bootstraps and get on with his life.

First of all, there was a widow he needed to see and a little boy who needed to know that his daddy was a hero. *Weber, I'll make sure your family is okay.*

PART TWO

Chapter Six

Two months passed and for Kyle it made a world of difference. Physical therapy had restored his ability to walk with the aid of the prosthesis. While it wasn't the same as having both of his own legs, it helped him move on with his life. With long pants on, he could almost forget that he had only one good leg. His arm was a different story. He had worked to be able to use the prosthetic arm, but no matter how much he tried, the damn hand wasn't the same as his own. It proved difficult to grip anything with that stupid thing and, in the end, it made him more frustrated than not having it.

Dressed, he pulled down the pant leg to cover his prosthesis. He was getting comfortable with it but he still preferred to keep it hidden from sight. Only around the house did he ever wear shorts and even that was rare. Staci had seemed to accept him for the man he was now. Maybe it was the fact she hadn't known him before the accident that made it easier. Either way, all that mattered was—they had bonded.

They'd gotten close in a friendship way and there were times when he wanted more, but he refused to act on it. Even though he had quit calling himself a cripple, he couldn't get past the fact she deserved someone better than him. He was broken.

As if his thought provoked her to call to him, her voice drifted across the hall toward his room. "You ready?"

"Just about." He grabbed his wallet from the nightstand and slipped it into his pocket before donning his watch. The idea of meeting Staci's friend from back home had him slightly on edge. While he had tried to be more social over the last few weeks, mostly chatting with some of the other local injured warriors, tonight he was completely out of his element.

It would be the first time he faced a stranger who didn't know his past. While he might be able to hide his prosthetic leg, he could do nothing about his arm or the burns. The latter made him the more self-conscious of the two. They ran nearly the length of his side. A few of the flames had licked the side of his face, leaving scars along his ear and cheek. The worst was hidden below his shirt, down his chest, and across his hip.

He looked at himself in the mirror. There had been changes over the months since the explosion, some for the better, while others he was still in the process of accepting. His military buzz cut had started to grow out, adding a little extra length to the top while he kept the sides tight. The burn scars had healed and added a certain ruggedness to his appearance. But it was the added muscle he had started to build since his injuries that proved the most surprising. As his way of working through things he had taken to the gym and learned exercises he could do with his new condition.

He grabbed his keys from the dresser and sighed. "Avoidance of social interactions will only make future ones harder."

The phone rang in the distance. He turned from the mirror just as she called out that she'd get the phone. He made it to the door in time to see her scurry down the hall toward the living room. She had a habit of leaving her cell phone on the entryway table, but the house was cozy enough that, if the volume was up, it could be heard through the house. With all the times the ringtone had interrupted them, he still hadn't decided whether that was a good or bad thing.

The evenings had become their time. It didn't matter what they did, but they spent them together. Sometimes they'd watch movies, play cards, board games, or just sit and talk. No matter what they did, it was special to him. He had grown closer to her than he had with anyone before. He had shared things with her that he had never told anyone else, not even Weber. Growing closer had made him want her more, as well. She was an amazing woman and as selfish as it seemed, he wanted her all to himself. He wanted her in ways he had never wanted a woman. Not just sexually but as a companion to spend the rest of his life with.

"Is she okay?" The fear that prickled in her voice chilled his blood and had him closing the distance between them. "I...I understand. I'll be there as soon as I can. Keep me posted." She pulled the phone away from her ear and hit the end button.

"What is it? What happened?"

"M...Mom." Tears rolled down her face. "She's had a heart attack. I've got to go home. Surgery...open heart surgery."

He wrapped his arm around her and held her to him. "It's going to be okay."

After a few minutes, the tears stopped, and she pulled the pieces back together. "They're still doing tests so they're not sure how bad it is, but the doctor said it looks like surgery tomorrow. I've got to call Heather and let her know I can't make dinner."

"I'll let her know while you pack. I'll make flight reservations and we'll leave right away."

"We?" She tipped her head up at him. Surprise filled her whiskey brown eyes, making them at least two shades darker.

"I'm not letting you make this trip alone. If you don't want me there, that's fine, but I'll see you to Tennessee until you're surrounded by family and friends. You're in no condition to travel by yourself." He rubbed his hand down her arm. "You once told me to let you help me and now I'm asking for you to do the same."

"There's no one else I'd rather have at my side. I just thought…you're meeting with some of the guys from base tomorrow."

"They'll understand; you're more important. Now go pack and I'll call Heather and get us reservations for the first flight out." She stepped back and looked at him. The tears had streaked her face and ruined her makeup but to him, she was beautiful.

"Thank you."

He watched as she dashed down the hall before picking up her discarded cell phone to find Heather's number. He'd call her first to cancel their dinner plans, make reservations, and then check on Staci again to make sure she was okay enough to pack. He could tell from her reaction that, even though she and her mother had their differences, she was taking the news hard. It might be hard for him to comprehend the connection between a parent and child, but he could see the pain in her eyes. That was enough to want to stand up and fight whatever had caused it. He cared about her deeply and didn't like to see her unhappy.

Admit it, you've fallen for her.

The plane ride had been uneventful and even checking into the hotel a few blocks away from the hospital did little to ease Staci's fears. She knew Colin, her mother's lover, was with her. Even though the two weren't legally married, they were bound like married couples. Colin had tried for the last several years to get her mother to marry him, but she refused. It had only been recently that Staci had uncovered the true reason. Her mother hadn't wanted to marry again because she was still in love with her father. Even though death and years had separated them, her mother remained deeply devoted to her husband. Sweet in a weird sort of way. Yet, she loved Colin in her own way.

"Why don't you call him? You can get an update and let him know you arrived." Kyle sat their suitcase next to the dresser in the hotel room. They had thrown everything into one to avoid the additional luggage charges as they flew. "Maybe with an update, you can get some rest."

From the room she could see the hospital buildings and through the darkness the lights glowed bright as a beacon. "Mom was always disappointed that I went away to college when the University here was just as good. That was almost a bigger fight than my major or the horse ranch. Now I'm only a few days away from graduation and she won't even see it."

"Don't say that." He came to stand next to her at the window and wrapped his arm around her shoulders. "Everything you've told me about your mother says she's a strong woman. She's going to get through this."

She leaned into his embrace and pressed her head against his shoulder. "Thank you for coming with me."

"I'd do anything for you."

"I better call him and let him know we arrived." Without stepping out of his embrace, she pulled her cell phone from her pocket and dialed Colin's number. It rang without any answer until it finally went to voicemail. "Colin, it's Staci. I've arrived and checked into the hotel room. Since I won't be able to get in to see her tonight I'm going to get some sleep and I'll be there in the morning to see the doctors. Call me if things change." She ended the call and slipped it back into her pocket. "Guess there's nothing to do but wait."

"You need some sleep. That will pass the time." He led her toward one of the two queen size beds in the room.

Under the stress, her thoughts seemed to want to focus on anything besides what was happening to her mother when they chose this hotel room.

He had asked for two adjoining rooms but this was all that was available. They could have gone to another hotel, but this one was the closest. She couldn't help but wonder if this wasn't the ultimate tease. Here she was sharing a room with a man she couldn't chase from her thoughts but remained off limits to her.

The way he ran his fingers down her arm made her reassess the situation. It wasn't she couldn't touch him rather she refused to allow herself to pressure him in that way. He had enough going on and while he had come a long way, a relationship shouldn't be top priority right now.

"I should change."

He nodded and let his arm fall from around her. "Yeah, it's been a long day."

Without his simple touches, she felt alone and the fear flooded back. Her mother was all she had left and she didn't want to lose her. With a deep breath, she forced herself to go to the suitcase and grab what she needed. A little bit of space between them, even just for the few minutes it would take her to change and wash her face, would allow her to regain control of her emotions. She wanted him now more than ever because she needed the comfort she'd find in his embrace.

A few minutes later, she strolled from the bathroom wearing only a tank top and shorts. Her thoughts had become more jumbled than before. She wanted to ask him to hold her, even if just for another moment. To be back in his embrace and have him dispel all her fears would stop her heart from thumping against her chest like a jackrabbit.

"Come here." Stretched out on the bed, the covers already pulled down, he held his good arm out to her, beckoning her.

She wanted to deny it, to tell him she was okay, but that would have been a lie. He knew what she needed and offered it freely. Without too much hesitation, she slipped onto the bed and curled up against him, so his arm wrapped around her back. "Thank you." She blinked away the tears as she found that special place in the crook of his arm to rest her head on.

"There's no need." He squeezed her tighter to him and placed a soft kiss on the crown of her head. "Try to rest."

Rest? How was she supposed to do that when her thoughts spun from the kiss? It wasn't like a kiss on the lips but it rattled her nonetheless. Did he feel something for her besides friendship? Or was she reading into his support and comfort? *Please don't let me start imagining things that are not there.*

Chapter Seven

The phone call came a few hours before dawn, drawing Staci from Kyle's warm embrace. It had taken her a few moments to realize where they were and what had happened but the minute she had, it all rushed back to her. The phone call had only brought worst news. Her mother had suffered a second heart attack and surgery would happen within the hour.

Not bothering to go into the bathroom, she slipped off her shorts and into a pair of jeans. She had to get to the hospital to see her mother before they took her in for surgery. Grabbing a sweater and bra from the bag, she headed for the bathroom. While she might have felt comfortable enough to change her bottoms, since everything was hidden behind her bright pink bikini panties, she wasn't going to pull off her tank top and show him her breasts. *Not yet at least.*

She had just pulled up her hair into a ponytail when Kyle's voice came from the other side of the bathroom door. "Fresh coffee is waiting."

She pulled her sweater over her head and pulled the door open to find him standing there enjoying his own cup of coffee. He was dressed in jeans and a blue button down shirt. "You didn't have to get up."

"I'm not going to have you sitting around the hospital for hours by yourself." He sat his mug aside and picked up a second one to hold out to her.

"Colin will be there," she reasoned, taking the coffee from him.

"But he's not me." A smirk spread across his face before a trace of doubt crept into his eyes. "Unless you'd rather I didn't."

"Don't be silly." She took a sip and it helped to wake her up the rest of the way. "I just meant you have to be tired. We barely got any sleep and I don't know how long I'll be there."

"Doesn't matter. I've come here to be with you, not stay in some hotel room. I'd rather be sleep deprived and with you than here wondering what was happening." He took another long drink of his brew, finishing it, before setting it on the kitchenette counter. "I'm ready if you are."

She took a few more quick gulps and sat hers aside as well. "Let me just grab my bag."

Fifteen minutes later, they were walking down the hospital corridors to her mother's room. From her volunteer work, she had grown used to hospitals but this time was different. She was there not to visit someone she barely knew, but for her mother. That thought iced her veins and made her stomach want to revolt.

"Staci..." Colin's words died off as he noticed Kyle. "Who's he?"

"Colin, meet Kyle. Kyle, this is my mother's friend, Colin." She did the introductions quickly so she could get to the real reason they were there. "How is she?"

"It's serious, but she has one of the best heart surgeons in Tennessee."

"Sir." A nurse stepped out of the room directly behind Colin. "You can go in now."

"Come on, they're taking her for surgery soon." Colin turned on his heels.

When she tried to follow, the nurse stopped her. "Excuse me, only family is permitted in there at this time."

"I'm her daughter." When the nurse looked to Kyle, she added, "My fiancé and if he's not allowed in there, then Colin shouldn't be either considering he's not family by any means." She knew she sounded snippy and as her mother would say, she'd have caught more bees with honey than vinegar, but she wasn't in the mood to deal with this. She wanted Kyle with her and she'd go to whatever lengths necessary, even pissing off her mother and Colin.

"Very well, but don't upset her."

As the nurse moved away, he leaned in close. "Fiancé? Wow, how things have progressed."

"Keep quiet or I'll have security boot you to the curb," she teased.

As much as she thought she was, she hadn't been prepared to step into her mother's room. To find the strong woman she knew in the hospital bed, her pale face drawn and all the wires, proved almost too much. *She's going to be okay,* she tried to reminder herself, but panic rose within her. Kyle wrapped his arm around her waist, his fingers pressed tight against her hip as if to cement her in the moment instead of being carried off with fear.

"Daughter, it's nice that my heart attack brought you home after months of being away."

Staci ground her teeth and refused to be bated. "Mother, you know with college, work, and everything else, things have been busy. I promised to visit once I finished."

"I see you brought a man home with you. Unscrupulous timing though. You can send him away now."

"Mother." She was embarrassed by her behavior. After everything Kyle had done for her, to have her mother treat him like that was beyond rude. "Kyle was nice enough to come here and support me. I won't have you being disrespectful. Now, Mom, why don't you tell me what the doctor said?"

"Oh, no. We're not going to gloss over your friend." Her mother pressed the button on the bed to raise it. "Come a little closer so I can get a better look. What did you say his name was?"

"Kyle." She tried to keep her patience but right now discussing Kyle was the least important thing. Her mother was about to have surgery and she wasn't even sure of the full extent of things.

"It's nice to meet you, Mrs. Pence." Kyle forced them to step closer to the bed.

"My daughter always wants to fix everyone." She shook her head. "But no matter how much you fix him you can't help him regain his arm. You don't even have the common sense you were born with. Stupid child."

"Mother!" Tears welled in her eyes. Kyle went still beside her.

"I might agree that Staci's timing to bring a man home is unfortunate but that was out of line." Colin stepped close to the bed.

"I'm only pointing out the obvious. She must have picked him up at that dreadful hospital."

"Ma'am, my injuries cost me more than I care to discuss, but they also brought an amazing woman into my life." He glanced down at Staci. "I care for your daughter, and while you may say what you'd like about me, there's no reason to disrespect her. She has traveled many hours to be here with you."

"You bring a man home with you in an emergency and you didn't even tell me you were seeing anyone. Or did you just pick up the first man you found in order to get me off your back?"

"Mom, this is not the time."

"I think it is." Her mother took a deep breath. "I'm about to go in for major open heart surgery, I think I'm entitled to know if my daughter is screwing…"

"That's enough." She decided to go with the same line she'd told the nurse, even though she'd have to build another lie later to cover up this one. "I didn't tell you before but we've been seeing each other for some time now. He's my fiancé. So have some respect."

"A son-in-law who won't even stand up for himself…that's not what I pictured as a husband for you. What kind of work can he possibly do with one arm?"

"Ma'am, I can fight my own battles, but considering the circumstances, it would be unwise to upset you further."

"Mrs. Pence, we're ready for you in pre-op." A gentleman in scrubs came into the room, followed by the nurse from before.

"Very well. It would seem that you're saved by the medical staff, but don't think this conversation is finished."

"I wouldn't think that for a moment." She knew she should go to the bed and hug or kiss her mother one last time but anger stopped her. She was tired of all of it and her mother's comments weren't just flung at her but also at Kyle. "I'll see you in recovery."

"You better make it out of surgery just fine." Colin leaned toward her mother and gave her a light kiss. "I love you, even when you're a bitch to those around you."

"Which is too often for my taste," Staci mumbled as she and Kyle left the room. The three of them would make their way to the surgery waiting room, but before Colin joined them, she wanted a moment alone with Kyle. She needed to apologize for her mother's actions.

Out in the hall, she led them away from that dreaded hospital room, and the path they'd take to get her mother to the operating room. With the hour, it wasn't difficult to find a quiet spot. "I'm so sorry."

"Don't." He leaned against the wall and brought her to stand in front of him. He wrapped his good arm around her waist while the one he'd partially lost touched her other side. "Her behavior isn't something I haven't encountered before and it won't be the last time. I chose not to wear my arm prosthesis today and maybe that made her more uncomfortable about my condition, but it was my decision. One that, even with her comments, I don't regret. I don't care for the prosthetic arm and feel I get along fine without it. You don't seem to mind it either, or I'd wear it. You also don't shy away from my stumps."

"I don't care if you choose to go without it and there's not one part of you that bothers me. You're sweet and I care about you, but her behavior is inexcusable. I understand if you wish to go back to the hotel, or even back home."

"I'm not leaving you." He rubbed a hand along the curve of her back. "I will say that, with the comments about me being your fiancé, you owe me. I'll wait to cash in until we're alone, but don't think I'll forget."

"Sorry about that, I just wasn't sure what else to say. I didn't want the nurse to force you to stay in the waiting room, and then when Mom started it also seemed for the best."

"You're apologizing for a lot of things out of your control. There's no need. I told you everything is going to be fine, though I have a feeling your mother doesn't like me very much."

"Don't worry, she doesn't like me either." She smirked. "I couldn't get through this without you."

"Don't underestimate yourself. You could, but it wouldn't be nearly as exciting." He laced his fingers through hers. "Come on, *fiancé*. I've a feeling Colin is waiting to question us some more on your mother's behalf."

"Colin owns a dozen or so horses that he races. It's how he and Mom met. They've been together for years and he's completely devoted to her. So there's no doubt he'll be getting whatever scoop he can find on us to report back to her."

"I'll let you take the lead and decide how much you want to give him."

They were just a few doors from the waiting room when she whispered. "How childish would it be if I said nothing?" She gave a lighthearted laugh. "I'm just tired of the way she pries into my life and tries to control it."

She wasn't completely sure what was happening between them, but it was special and she didn't want to share it with anyone. Let alone have it examined under a microscope by her mother until she could find additional fault in it.

Mom, I think I love him. If you knew that, you still wouldn't be happy for me.

She knew better than to let her mother know about her feelings toward Kyle. No one had been good enough to gain her mother's permission. She hadn't even liked any of Staci's friends, the only one she tolerated was Heather, and that had been after years of their friendship. Heather had a way with people and people opened up to her. It's what made her a good therapist.

Thoughts of Heather had Staci make a mental note to call her best friend later. She had come into town, almost especially to see Staci and then this happened. It wasn't her fault, but she felt bad about the unfortunate timing. She'd have to make it up to Heather soon. Maybe a trip to see her was in order.

"I was wondering where you two disappeared to." Colin stood outside of the waiting room, as if waiting for them.

"I needed some air." She forced herself to smile even if she only mustered a halfhearted one. The issue wasn't that she didn't like Colin—because she did—but more the fact that everything she ever said to the man had been reported back to her mother. This wasn't entirely his fault. She knew all too well how her mother was; the woman wouldn't give in until she knew every dirty detail, no matter how small.

"Your mother isn't happy about your companion."

She advanced on him until Kyle touched her shoulder. "I love my mother, but my personal life is my own business."

"You make it our business when you bring that *personal life* to a family emergency."

"Mother's training you well," she spat. "You're even getting her lethal tongue. But I'll tell you this, he's more family than she has ever been. I was never good enough for her. Nothing I ever did was what she wanted me to do, and once my father died, it only got worse. I love her, but I realized that my life is just that, *mine*. I need to live it on my terms. It's the reason I moved away for college. It's also the reason why, once I'm finished, I won't be returning home."

"Your mother and I are already aware of your plans to buy that filthy ranch in Kentucky."

"For someone who owns and raced horses, you sure don't get it." She took in the man before her and realized one thing. In the last several years, he had changed. No longer was he wearing jeans, a flannel shirt, and a cowboy hat. Even at the early hour, he stood before her looking ready to head to a business meeting. His dress pants looked only slightly wrinkled, matched with a fresh, crisp shirt and the tie firmly in place. "Mom changed you into the man she wanted."

"That was my business, not my passion. I did it for the money I made, and if I've changed, it's been for the better."

"I'm not so sure about that." Tired of having to defend her actions, she stepped past him and into the waiting room.

"Staci…" He waited until she turned to look at him, a nasty grin on his face. "That horrid ranch you love so much will be sold soon and you'll lose your chance. The best thing is, I played a part in the old man's decision to sell. Your mother will be so pleased once that idea is out of your head and you can finally grow up. Stop living a dead man's dream."

Chapter Eight

Kyle wrapped his arm around Staci before she could do or say something she might regret. Colin had been trying to provoke her and the way her body vibrated with anger warning Kyle he was about to succeed. Unlike with Mrs. Pence's sharp tongue, he knew she'd lash out in a more personal way and right now wasn't the time for it. "Come with me."

"I need to stay here. What if the doctor comes back?"

"No, you need to come with me. We won't be far and the doctor will find you. After all, you're her next of kin. He won't be able to give the news to *anyone* else." He eyed the other man, making clear what he meant: that the doctor wouldn't be able to give the surgery update to him without her there.

He kept his arm tight around her, leading her from the waiting room, and a little ways down the hall. When he came to a stop, she leaned against the wall and let out a growl. He wanted to hold her tight, to ease the pain and stress that boiled within her. "Deep breaths."

"Why do I let them get under my skin?" She wiped a tear that had rolled down her face. "It was stupid…I thought after all this time away maybe things had changed. That they'd accept me for the person I am rather than the one Mom wants me to be, but that's never going to happen. This proves it. They can't even let it go in a situation like this."

"My instinct is to tell you that you should live for yourself. To make yourself happy, not someone else. If this ranch means so much to you, then continue on the path you're on. Don't let their comments sway you from your dreams." He took her hand into his. "But maybe I'm not the one to listen to. What do I know about families?"

"Oh, Kyle."

"I don't want your pity," he reminded her. "I only meant maybe this is the normal interaction within families. I was never a part of one long enough to know. What I do know is that life is precious, and you have to live every minute to the fullest. We never know when our ticket will be punched, so you have to follow your dreams." For a moment, his thoughts returned to the day they deployed. Weber's wife and son standing there to see him off. All of Weber's dreams that would never get fulfilled now. He had to force those memories back and focus on the woman before him, who he could still help.

"It wasn't like this until after Dad died. Before that, Mom and I might not have seen eye to eye but we didn't fight every time we were in the same room with each other. Once Dad wasn't there as a buffer between us it all went to Hell. I swear she hates me because I'm not like her. She doesn't like that I'm different than her, or that I don't value the same things. She sees me spreading my wings and believes I'm doing it in spite of her instead of because it's what I want. You know, since I moved away to get my Master's degree, I've been home once in two years."

"Going home can be hard. Everyone around you expects you to be who you were when you left but you come back a different person." That was something he could relate to because he remembered the few days' leave he'd had before they deployed. He'd wanted to see his hometown one last time in case he didn't make it back. While he was there he ran into some people he knew, including his old case manager, who had placed him in countless foster care homes. They had expected him to be the goof off kid he had been when he left, but he had changed.

"Now, everything I've worked for might be gone." She leaned forward and rested her head on his chest. "All I ever wanted was that ranch."

"Maybe he's just talking to upset you."

She shook her head against his chest. "Mr. Cline has been talking about selling the place. It's becoming too much for him. He knows I've always wanted to own it and was supposed to give me a call if he ever wanted to sell. Since my first job, I've been putting all my extra money aside in order to buy it, but there's no way I have enough saved. Not yet."

"If he was supposed to call you and you haven't heard from him then maybe it's just talk. Either way, we'll find out."

"Mr. Cline's word is good, but if someone got to him with an offer he couldn't refuse, that could explain why he didn't let me know."

Not knowing what else to do, he wrapped his arms around her and just held her. He'd find out the truth about the ranch but if there was already a contract signed like Colin implied, there'd be little he could do. Maybe there was another horse ranch she'd be happy with. Though he doubted this because for her it wasn't just about owning a horse ranch. It was the memories made with her father at Cline's ranch that made the place so special to her. The bond she'd had with her father had been transferred to the ranch when he died.

"It's stupid to be standing in the hallway all upset about a piece of land when my mother is having surgery, but it feels like I've lost Dad all over again."

"I know, sugar." He held her tighter and tried not to think that he had just called her sugar. He didn't want to contemplate what that meant. Rather, he focused on having her in his arms—something he had wanted to do for a while now. He'd have preferred this to happen under other circumstances but since he had denied himself her touch before, he'd take it any way he could get it.

The surgery turned out to be a success and now there was nothing to do but wait. Alone in the waiting room, Staci cuddled against Kyle. It had been a long, stressful twenty-four hours and all she wanted to do was go back to the hotel and sleep. One last visiting session of the night and she could do just that.

Colin had disappeared a little more than an hour before in search of dinner, but there was no doubt he'd be back for the visit. She wanted to deny him the right to see her mother, just out of spite because of his comments throughout the day. If he wasn't making a comment about her or Kyle, it was the ranch, or how she disappointed her mother. It had gotten to be too much.

How long was she expected to stay in Tennessee? Too long, and she'd lose her mind. If Mom's recovery went as planned, she'd be released in a few days, and Staci could return home. Yet, she wasn't sure what going home would mean because suddenly, she felt lost. Everything she had worked for was gone. She'd taken this trip because her mother was sick and ended up grieving for her father and the ranch. It didn't seem right but sometimes emotions weren't something that could be changed.

She also had no idea how things would stand between her and Kyle when they returned home. Something between them had changed since they arrived. It felt right to be in his embrace, to be cuddled against him, and not just because she claimed they were engaged. *Engaged.* She'd have some serious explaining to deal with later, but the announcement had made this trip easier. The next trip would be hellish, but that would be the price she'd pay.

"I see the two of you are exactly where I left you." Colin strolled toward them.

She couldn't keep the moan from escaping. "Colin, we never had this much of an issue last time I visited, so do you want to tell me what changed? Why do you suddenly seem to hate me?"

"We were never close, so it's not that big of a change." He sank down into a chair across from them, crossed his arms over his chest, and stared at her.

"True but you didn't despise me. Unlike my mother, I can't see you having a fit like this because I brought my fiancé home for a family emergency. So what's the issue? Because as of right now I've had it."

"Your father might have bought that innocent act but I don't and neither does your mother."

"What's that supposed to mean?"

"Stac—" Kyle started.

"No, it's okay. I want to hear whatever issue he has with me."

"Your mother cares for you more than you know. She finally told me why she won't marry me." The heat in his gaze was directed at her as if she was supposed to know.

"What the hell are you talking about? Why would her reasoning be my fault?"

"She won't marry me because of you." He leaned forward and clasped his hands in front of him. "Marrying me would drive the two of you further apart than you already are. You're so devoted to your father's memory that you'd see our marriage as a betrayal to him. She told me you warned her that if we marry you'll cease all contact with her."

She sat there, her mouth agape, unable to believe him. She couldn't decide if she was more upset at her mother for telling such lies or at Colin for believing them. *Boy, these two idiots were made for each other.* Lies had always been a part of her mother getting her own way, but this was taking things to an extreme. Lies between lovers doomed a relationship but for some reason she didn't suspect Colin of going anywhere. He seemed completely devoted to her mother.

"Man, you actually believe that?" Kyle spoke before she could even wrap her thoughts around everything Colin said.

"Stay out of this. It's a family issue."

"No, he's right. I can't believe you swallowed that line. Mom has twisted things to meet her own needs before, but I've never had a problem with you.

Dad died years ago and it was barely a year after his death that she started dating you. All these years she's controlled things when it came to both of us. I moved away to escape and what? She sank her claws deeper into you? So much that you actually believed *I* was the reason she wouldn't marry you."

"Are you telling me that's not true?" Colin stood and walked around to the back of his chair.

"Damn right I am. Mom deserves to be happy and last time I was home it seemed that you made her happy." Her mother had given her a reason why she didn't want to marry Colin but now that she heard what *he* was told, what could the truth be? Maybe none of it was true. Whatever her rationale, Colin needed to be the one to find out. Their relationship didn't concern her.

"Whatever the reason is, it's not Staci's fault," Kyle pointed out.

She glanced at him and then back to her mother's man. "I think you need to talk to her. I've known for years you've wanted to marry her and I have no issues with that. Actually, I wish you all the best. You've got more courage and strength than I have to deal with her every day."

"We all have our faults." He squeezed the back of the chair. "I love her."

"I think we'll go back to the hotel." She slipped from Kyle's embrace and stood.

"What about the last visiting time?"

"I think you and Mom need to talk. I'll see her in the morning and if anything happens, you and the nurses have my number." She stifled a yawn. "I'm exhausted, but I'll be back in the morning to speak with the doctors."

"I'm not leaving, so if there's any change, I'll call you."

Admiring the love he had for her mother and how he wore it on his sleeve, she smiled at him. She truly hoped the two of them would work things out.

"The chairs in here aren't very comfortable but I hope you're able to get some sleep. Tomorrow she should be out of the ICU and in a private room so at least you won't have to be stuck in a waiting room."

She didn't wait for him to comment. She grabbed her bag and headed to the door, Kyle next to her. She needed to get to the hotel and recharge. The private room might be a benefit to Colin and his sleep, but it would do little for them all being together. The doctors had warned that Mom was not to be stressed. Tomorrow, it was going to prove difficult to accomplish that. Tonight, however, she needed to explore something different.

Kyle.

Chapter Nine

Kyle stepped back into the room after depositing the room service tray in the hallway for the staff to collect. Dinner had been okay but the company had seemed to have something on her mind and he was about to get to the bottom of it. It seemed more than just worry about her mother, or the crap Colin had said. Was she still upset about the ranch? He pulled his cell phone from his pocket and checked the screen. Nothing. Earlier in the day he had called a fellow injured vet, who had some crazy skills when it came to computers, to have him see what he could find out about the Cline ranch. He remembered the old saying, no news is good news, but he wasn't sure that was always the case.

He closed the door behind him and glanced to where Staci stood by the window. She tugged the cardigan tight around her, hiding the way the tank top curved to her body. Her hair hung down around her shoulders in soft cascading curls. She was beautiful. "Are you okay?"

"Fine." She glanced at him and shot him a halfhearted smile.

"Don't lie to me." He closed the distance to her. "Are you upset about Colin?"

"No, that's their business and they'll work it out." She turned away from the window to face him. "Am I imagining this?"

Inches from her, he wanted to reach out and caress her. "Imagining what?"

"This...*us*." Her cheeks burned red.

"Do you want to be imagining it?" He reached up and tucked a strand of hair behind her ear before letting his fingers travel down her neck, teasing softly along the curve of it. "Or do you want this?"

"I put you in a sensitive spot earlier with the fiancé comment, but we're alone now. If this is an act..."

"Is that what you want, for this to be an act?" He wanted her to say it. To say that she wanted him as badly as he wanted her. He hated feeling vulnerable—an emotion he hadn't experienced since he had come back from overseas in his current condition. All the time and work that had transpired since he woke up to find himself a cripple in the hospital, and now, in some ways, he felt like he had ended up back there. Only, this time, more vulnerable than ever.

"Stop returning each question with one of your own. I just want to know where we stand. I mean...I don't want there to be any confusion, any mixed signals."

"Mixed signals..." *So it had all been an act for her.* It might have been one for her but it sure hadn't been for him. He had started to fall for her nearly from the beginning. She had been in his thoughts since she strolled into his hospital room with her whiskey brown eyes, and her sweet country accent. "I think I'll go work out. You can think about your mixed signals and decide what you really want."

He went to the suitcase but stopped before grabbing workout clothes. What had he been thinking? He couldn't use a hotel gym. People would stare and while normally that would bother him, right now it would be like shoving a second knife though his back. He left the clothes and headed for the door. He needed to get out of there, to get air.

"Kyle..." she called to him as his good hand clenched the door handle and pulled it open.

He didn't stop, couldn't stop. He had to give himself time to think. Damn it, he loved her. Stepping into the hallway, he headed for the elevator. No car keys meant wherever he was going would have to be local. He didn't care where he ended up or how he got there; he just needed fresh air to clear his thoughts.

Falling in love with her had been the stupidest thing he had done yet. How could he ever think a woman like her would ever return his feelings? She could do better than him. While, for him, she was a dream. Not because he was a cripple but because of who she was. She saw him for more than his former military career and looked past his defects. He loved her and he never thought he'd have a woman like her in his life. Now, before they even had a chance, the dream was being tugged out of his hands and there was nothing he could do to stop it. Love isn't always enough…

It had been nearly two hours since Kyle had left and Staci couldn't stop pacing the small confines of the room. She had given him a few minutes to calm down and given herself the time to get her thoughts in order before she had tried to find him. She searched the hotel, the garden behind, even the couple of blocks around the hotel. After she looked everywhere she could think of and still came up empty, she was stuck waiting in the hotel for him to come back. She had the car keys and all his belongings; even his wallet and cell phone were tossed on the dresser. He couldn't have gone home, but she had no idea where he was.

Her chest felt tight and her stomach roiled. The conversation that had started all of this hadn't gone how she wanted and until he came back, she couldn't fix it. She could blame it on whatever she wanted, but the truth was, her own nerves had caused the misunderstanding. She was falling in love with him and the fiancé lie had pushed them over the unease and straight into a *relationship*. Only now, she wasn't sure where he stood. Did he have any feelings for her or was he just playing a game in order to help her get through this family visit? She needed to know his true meaning and if he felt anything besides friendship for her. That had been the reason behind why she had pushed the subject even after their conversation had started to take a disastrous turn.

"Where are you, Kyle?" She tugged the cardigan tight around her and moseyed to the window. She considered going back out to check the area for him but each time, she stopped herself. He'd come back when he was ready. He'd have to. She tried to reassure herself, but it wasn't working. She needed to apologize, to explain she was an idiot. She wasn't used to all the emotions that were rolling around within her. It would have been a hell of a ride even without the family drama added in.

She pulled back the curtain and there, midway in the garden, she could just barely make out a figure sitting on a bench. Not just any figure—but Kyle. She slipped her feet into her shoes and went to the door. If he wasn't coming in, then she'd go to him. Two hours was more than enough time for him to think, and it had also been long enough for her to realize what an idiot she had been.

She grabbed the hotel key card and dashed from the room. Seeing others in the hall, she didn't take off in a run as she wanted; instead, she hastened her walk, taking the shortest route to him. Skipping the elevator, she took the steps, jogging down them, and doubts crept in as she went. What if he didn't feel the same way as she did?

You won't know unless you try. At least then she'd know one way or another. If he didn't feel anything but friendship for her, then she needed to end things before it broke her heart even more. She'd make some excuse for him to return home, while she stayed here to care for her mother. This would be the only way, because she couldn't continue pretending to be engaged to him when he felt nothing for her.

Stepping out into the night's air, the wind whipped her hair into her face. The cool chill pressing against her did nothing to diminish the heat pouring through her at the sight of him just ahead, on the same bench she had seen him at from the window. As still as a statue, he leaned against the arm rest with his head in his hand.

"Kyle…" She paused, hoping he would look up or even say something, but he did neither. "I'm sorry for what I said before. For the mixed signals—"

"Don't," he growled, still not looking at her. "Just forget it all. I don't want to hear it."

She caught the rise in his tone. "It?"

"Yes. How you're sorry that you led me on but you could never be with a cripple like me. I don't need or want your pity."

"Damn it, Kyle." Wanting to see his face, she sank to her knees in front of him. "That's not what I'm sorry for. So, if you'd just hear me out…" When he remained silent, she laid her hand on his leg and wished he'd look at her. "I'm sorry that I questioned what was happening. I couldn't believe that your…behavior wasn't just an act to keep up with the fiancé statement. I didn't want to lead myself on to only have my heart broken."

"So you'd rather give in to doubts than listen to your heart," he stated as if it was that easy. "Because I could have done the same but instead, I ignored those uncertainties. Maybe I was wrong."

"Kyle." She reached up and cupped his face, feeling the contours of his injuries under her fingers, and it broke her heart all he had gone through. The marred skin, puckered up in places from the burns, deep grooves in others. But all this comprised only part of what lay beneath his clothes. To her, the scars didn't matter. To her, he'd never been the cripple or freak he saw himself as. "I…I…oh hell." She forced herself to take a deep breath and let it out slow. "Somewhere along the way, I've fallen in love with you."

He finally glanced up at her, his eyes burning with the heat of his rage. "I don't need your pity, Staci. You don't need to love the cripple to make him feel better or so he'll stay here and keep up the pretenses with your family."

"Kyle…" She couldn't keep the tears from sliding down her face. This wasn't the special *I love you* moment she had dreamed about. It was now obvious that he didn't care for her. "It's not because of pity or because of what I told my family. If I had been willing to admit it, I'd have told you days ago, but I didn't think you were ready or heck, even interested in me."

She'd come out here wanting to make things right but it seemed like she was only making them worse. How delusional was she for thinking he'd wrap his arm around her and hold her tight, but she'd be damned if that wasn't what she wanted. "It's too cold to sit here. Come back inside. I'll leave you alone if that's what you want, but please, come inside. In the morning, if you want to leave, I'll understand."

"I wouldn't leave you to deal with your family alone."

She noticed he hadn't said he wanted to stay. Only that he'd stay out of some duty to her. "Only if you want to be here. I'll deal with Mom if I need to, and maybe things will be different with Colin."

The rage that had been in his eyes moments before was now replaced by sadness. "I care for you more than I should. You deserve someone better than a cripple."

"Stop that. You're not…"

"Bullshit," he interrupted her before she could finish. "I'm missing two limbs and I have burns down my body. While you might be able to forget about the leg, you can't forget about this." He held up his arm to where the stump was just barely covered by his long sleeved dress shirt.

"I don't care about any of that, and whether or not you return my feelings. I love you for you. Your appearances or injuries don't play into that. You're handsome in a rugged sort of way and damn, do I find that sexy." She touched his injured arm and he started to pull away from her. "Why don't you wear the prosthetic arm?"

"You know why."

"No, I don't. Sure, I said many get to the point where they don't want it. But everyone has their own reasons. The technology for the bionic limbs is better than it was before, and there are body-powered or electric-powered prosthetics. Is it because you don't want to learn to work them?"

"They're not the same. I've used them. Hell, you know I have one. The damn things are a pain in the ass. Not because of the training they take but because it's not the same. To hold you with one wouldn't be the same as holding you with both of my arms. With those damn prosthetics I can't pretend that I have both of my arms and this way…" He glanced down at his injured arm. "I'm always reminded of my limitations."

"But you're not limited. Do you remember the night you hugged me and touched me with your injured arm? I didn't shy away because I don't see you as injured. You're just a man; a man I've come to care about. I was trying to say that before but it got all messed up."

"Care about as a friend." Sadness laced his words.

"As a friend but also more than that. Kyle, I'm in love with you."

He took hold of her wrist and pulled her up onto the bench next to him. "You deserve so much better than me."

"Think what you will, but it's you I want." She leaned her head against his shoulder. "Come back inside."

Just as Colin and her mother needed to work things out, she and Kyle had to do the same thing. Only, she didn't want to do so sitting out in the cold. She had told him how she felt and needed to know where things stood with him. She wasn't asking for a commitment or some life altering declaration. An expression of his feelings toward her would be enough and they could move forward however they wished and on their own time schedule. If he felt nothing for her, then she'd accept it, but she had to know.

Kyle lay stretched out beside Staci as she cuddled against his good side, his arm gently rubbing along her back. They had slept cuddled together as if they thought the morning light would change everything. Now awake, he still couldn't believe she actually had feelings for him. She could have any man she wanted and instead, she wanted him, despite him being a disfigured cripple. He should have had the strength to walk away from her, to let her live a life without always having people stare at them because of his scars, but he couldn't bring himself to do it.

The way her body pressed against his, as if she had been built to fit snuggly against him, had been the final straw. He needed her like he needed air for his lungs. She had strolled into his hospital room and saved him. With each day, she continued to give him the strength he needed to push forward.

As much as he wanted her, there were lingering doubts in the back of his mind that one day she'd leave him for someone who wasn't a cripple. Someone who wouldn't scare small children. More to the point, someone who wouldn't wake up in a cold sweat from the nightmares that haunted him.

"You're thinking too much. Doubting this." She rubbed her hand along his chest.

Unable to meet her gaze, he closed his eyes. "You deserve better than me."

"You said that before but this is my choice. You're my choice." She let her hand travel up his chest to brush it against his chin. "Don't let the doubt take up residency in your thoughts. We deserve a chance."

He wasn't sure what he would have said to that but his phone vibrated before he had to come up with a reply. "I should get that."

"I guess I should shower. Then breakfast and the hospital."

He hated for her warm body to leave his side but he suspected this was the phone call he had been waiting for. "I'll order breakfast once I've dealt with this." He slipped his arm from around her and reached over to grab his cell phone off the nightstand. As his hand wrapped around the phone, he realized it wasn't a call but a text message. *Sale fell through this morning. If interested call...*

The phone number for Mr. Cline followed.

"Everything okay?" She slipped off the other side of the bed and went to the suitcase.

"Better than okay." He grabbed the hotel stationery and jotted down the number. "I've got to return this call."

She nodded and headed toward the bathroom to shower and get ready. When he heard the water running, he quickly dialed the number. It was early but he didn't want to miss the opportunity. If the sale had fallen through, there might be another buyer waiting in the woodwork ready to place an offer.

On the third ring, a rough voice answered. "Cline residence."

"Good morning, Mr. Cline. I'd like to talk to you about buying your ranch."

Chapter Ten

The next two days were spent going back and forth from the hospital to the hotel. In the midst of it all, Kyle still managed to work out the details with Mr. Cline. Nearly everything was in order. The only thing that stood in the way of the closing in three weeks was a visit to tour the land and sign the remaining paperwork. That had to happen tomorrow or the deal was off. This would give the Clines the retirement they wanted and Staci the ranch she had dreamed about since she was a child. It made him slightly nervous that he hadn't told her anything about the deal, but he wanted this to be a surprise—his way of giving something back to her for all she had done for him.

The days had also given him a different perspective on her. While she loved her mother, she was stressed out more when they were together. The two women were so different, they clashed in nearly every way. Even with Colin and him there to act as buffers, the hours spent at the hospital had some sticky moments where the women had drawn their claws.

Whatever had happened after her heart surgery, Mrs. Pence and Colin seemed to have a newly developed tension between them. Had they not worked out the issue of marriage or was it something else? Either way, it wasn't his business and Staci didn't seem too interested in digging further.

"What's on your mind?" Staci sat across from him, picking at her grilled chicken salad.

"I've got something to tell you…something I wanted to keep as a surprise until things were final, but I can't figure out how to make tomorrow work otherwise."

"What's tomorrow?" She sat her fork aside.

He had wanted to plan a nice romantic dinner to tell her what he had done but that idea had been tossed out when her mother spiked a fever that morning. "I'm meeting Mr. Cline."

"Cline as in Cline ranch?" Her eyes widened.

He nodded. "I'm purchasing the place."

"What?" She leaned back against the booth, clearly angry. "You don't want the ranch. What do you know about horses? Or running a ranch?"

"Just calm down for a moment and let me explain." He reached across to her and took her hand in his. "I'm purchasing the ranch for you."

She blinked as if she tried to wrap her thoughts around what he just said. "Wait. Colin said that Mr. Cline had someone purchasing it."

"It fell through and now I'm buying it."

"But why?"

He smirked at the very idea of him owning the farm himself. "It's for you as a token of my appreciation for all you've done. You saved my life and for that I owe you a lot more than this ranch."

"You don't owe me anything."

"I want to do this." He squeezed her hand. "Mr. Cline needs to sell. He didn't call you because he knew you were still in college. He didn't want you to give it up just to come back to the ranch. He thought your father would roll over in his grave if he were the reason you quit school. That's the reason he didn't contact you, not because he didn't want you to own the place."

"Needs to retire." The surprise made her voice rise a notch.

"His wife has been ill for some time and the cold weather is too much for

84

her. They want to move to Florida where their daughter lives." He paused because this was the part he hadn't been sure he wanted to tell her or if he wanted to leave things be. "Colin pressured him into selling."

"He what?" She interrupted and started to slide from the booth. She shouldn't have been surprised after Colin's comments before but she was. She had tried to live in denial because it wouldn't have just been him but also her mother.

"Wait." He squeezed her hand a little tighter so she couldn't get away.

"I'm not sure how it all happened, but they were acquaintances from years in the horse industry and Colin mentioned that he might know someone who was interested. At first, Mr. Cline thought he meant you…" He trailed off at the pain in her eyes. "It doesn't matter how, but you should know the reasoning behind it. Colin thought if that ranch was no longer a possibility, you and your mother would move on and forget about that place and your father. He had hoped it would finally bring the possibility of them getting married to the forefront."

"That swine!" The surprise that had been in her voice was now replaced with anger and sadness.

"Come here." He tugged her hand until she got up and came around the table to sit on his side of the bench. He slipped his arm around her shoulders and cuddled her against him. "I know you're upset about what he did, but tomorrow we'll go tour the ranch, look over the books and ranch commitments. In three weeks, we will close and the place will be yours."

"No, it will be yours."

"I thought it was clear I'm not buying the ranch for me but for you."

"Why? I was supposed to work for this. I've been saving every dime I could to buy that place."

"Trust me, there's plenty of work for you to do," he teased. "No, seriously, I know how much this place means to you and how devastated you were when you thought you'd lost your chance to purchase it. I didn't want to see that happen again."

"How did you even know the deal fell through?" She tipped her head up to look at him.

"After Colin's announcement about snatching the ranch out from under you, I called a friend of mine. He did some research and contacted Mr. Cline. That's what the text message I received the other morning was about. Immediately, I called and placed a bid on it, so we didn't miss our chance." He lifted his hand from her shoulder and tangled it in her hair. "I know you wanted to buy it but weren't in the position yet. If it bothers you I purchased it for you, then consider me a business partner and when you're ready, buy me out."

"Why would you want to get involved in a horse ranch? You've even admitted you've never even been on a horse before."

"I did it for you. I know how much that place means to you. I couldn't stand by and let someone else own it." No, he couldn't, especially without knowing if they'd have the same devotion for it as she had. She loved that place and the memories that surrounded it and he loved *her*. As strange as it was, the ranch completed things.

"I'm having a hard time wrapping my mind around this. For days I've thought my chance of owning it was gone and now…" The first tear rolled down her face. "Thank you."

"You're welcome, sugar. Thank you for strolling into my life and saving me."

"We saved each other." She tipped her head to rest against his chest. "I wasn't living before you. I'd go to class, work, and the hospital, but that was it. Since Heather graduated and moved back to Kentucky, I've just been going through the motions of living. I never thought what is happening between us could…well, happen, but I'm glad it did."

"Me too."

"There's no polite way to ask this so I'll take a page from your book and just come out with it. Cline's ranch isn't just some dinky little place. I've been saving for years and still don't have the money. How can a Lance Corporal afford to drop the money needed on this ranch? Especially when it's not your dream but you're doing it for me."

"You know I was a foster care child without a dime to my name when I turned eighteen but it was a few months before I deployed things changed." He stared off and thought about the person that he didn't even know. "My biological mother's family had money, so much that my grandmother was able to bribe people to report to her as my life progressed. When she died, she left the money to me. The lady that gave birth to me tried to fight it but the suit was dropped while I was in the hospital. Honestly, I never cared about the money, never even touched it, but now it seems like it had a purpose after all."

"What about your mother? Have you had any contact with her?"

"No, and as far as I'm concerned, she's not my mother, just the woman who gave birth to me. There's no relationship beyond that. You have to do more for a child than that to be considered a parent." He let out a light chuckle. "Funny thing is, the family made their money racing horses."

"Maybe it's in your blood."

"Maybe." He kissed the top of her head. "I was intrigued a little and learned my father was a jockey that my mother was having an affair with. She kept the pregnancy a secret, hiding away in the house when it became obvious and her husband made excuses she was traveling. After she gave birth, I was whisked away."

"I'm sorry."

"Don't be. It brought us a new adventure. Tomorrow...I know it's bad timing with your mother's condition and this new infection so I understand if you don't wish to go with me, but I promised to meet with him."

"I'll go."

"Good, because like you already pointed out, what do I know about a horse ranch? I need you there to go over things with me, to check the books, and the commitments we'll be held to. I need you." Mentally he added, *in more ways than you know.*

He held her tight against him and enjoyed the moment. Tomorrow, they'd start a new journey together as ranch owners and he would have to begin learning what it took to run a place like that. Yet, just then, he only wanted to focus on Staci and the knowledge that lurked inside of him waiting for him to acknowledge it.

He wasn't simply falling in love with her; he was head over heels *in* love with her.

The next day came, as they always do, but not fast enough for Staci. Even as they sat in the rental car on their way to the ranch, she wanted to tell him to step on the gas pedal. It seemed like he was driving too slowly, and it was taking too long to get there. It had been years since she had been back to the area where she grew up and even longer since she had been at the ranch. Now, she was finally on her way and, while the place wasn't actually yet hers, the fulfillment of her dream loomed closer than ever.

The guilt from what she thought when Colin had told her the ranch was being sold still made her stomach turn. She had been so upset and unable to get that ranch out of her thoughts and during that time, she had thought some rather nasty things about Mr. Cline. His word had always been good, but when he didn't call to let her know he wanted to sell the ranch, that seemed to change her opinion about him. Now here she was about to own the place with Kyle.

Kyle had refused to discuss their business partner arrangements until after they saw the place, but she was determined to pay him back every cent. The ranch meant everything to her and he was doing this for her. She didn't want his act to be out of some misguided sense of indebtedness because he didn't owe her anything. This was her dream and somehow she had tugged him into it.

They made the turn onto the road that would lead them to the ranch and she sat up straighter, her heart beat faster. As they drove through the small town, she noticed everything looked different, but that was nothing compared to what the entrance into the ranch looked like. Beautiful big trees lined the road, with their bright green leaves, and brought back so many memories. Happy memories.

She refused to think of the winter when her mother had left the ranch and the area to move them to Nashville. Or how bare the trees had been with a light dusting of snow on the branches. That memory was too close to the day of her father's funeral. Winter held sadder memories—like the world was trying to do away with the old to make room for the new. Only her father wasn't the old and shouldn't have been taken from her on that cold winter's day.

"Your mood sure changed." He glanced over at her before returning his attention to the road.

"I was thinking of yesteryear and winter. The death of the land can bring the death of other things."

"Your father."

She reached across the space toward him and placed her hand on his leg. "I lost him in the winter and the following year, Mom forced us to move to Nashville. Said we couldn't live here any longer with his memories haunting us at every turn. It had been just over a year since his death and that move felt almost like losing him all over again. That was the last winter I lived here. I came back in the summers and when Mom needed a break, because the Clines were like grandparents to me, but it was never the same."

"This winter the place will be ours and we can make happy memories."

"I still can't believe it." She glanced back out the window. "My emotions are all mixed up at the moment. I'm happy to be here, thrilled with our new adventure, saddened by the negative memories this brings back of my father's death, and feeling ill at the thought of telling my mother."

"This is your life and you need to live it on your terms. You've done that with your degree, this ranch, and, well...me."

"You?"

"Mrs. Pence has never once tried to hide the fact that she's unhappy with *us*. She doesn't want you with some sorry excuse for a man."

"Kyle!" She slapped his leg. "I won't sit here while you use such a degrading term to refer to yourself. You're an amazing man."

"You see what you want to see and not the outer shell that everyone else can't get past. The point still is she isn't happy about this. Especially since she thinks I'm to be her son-in-law soon."

"I don't care what she thinks. I'm happy being with you."

"Wow. Look at this place."

She turned back to the road and noticed the white fences that marked the horse areas had disappeared and they were heading up the incline to the main house. The log ranch home stretched out wide so that every room had a view of the land. It was set up in such a way that two of the four bedrooms had views of both sides of the ranch. She remembered waking up on the mornings when she was visiting and looking out over the grounds. The master bedroom had more stunning views, not just on the front and back but also the side. The back end of the property overlooked the lake. Mr. Cline worked around the lake because his wife had refused to let him fill it in.

"Wait until you see inside." She smiled and let the memories wash over her. "On the other side of that barn you'll find the workers' quarters. He's never had a large staff, only one or two, but it's set up for six workers, each with their own living quarters and a shared kitchen. At least it was so last time I was here."

"According to what information I have, it still is. There's also a cabin a little farther behind where the ranch manager and his family live in. He's been with the Clines for years and now handles a lot of the stuff Mr. Cline used to do before his wife got sick. He was the main horse trainer before he took this current position. His son now works as trainer."

"Not Clifford. He can't still be here."

"Yeah, I think that's his name." He pulled the car in front of the main house and put it in park. "Do you know him?"

She nodded. "His son was just a kid last time I saw them. He can't be older than sixteen now."

"I'm not sure but I know he's being homeschooled." He nodded toward the house. "Ready?"

She glanced at the log home and nodded. "I still can't believe this is really happening."

"Believe it, sugar. In three short weeks, this will be our home and the ranch you've always dreamed of owning will be yours."

"Ours." She leaned toward him and pressed her lips to his. They were on this journey together. Business partners and so much more.

Chapter Eleven

Their tour of the ranch had some high and low points as it also brought to life what work needed to be done. Staci was excited to get her hands back into it, but going around the place had given her an idea she hadn't fully considered before. A way to make both her degree and the ranch work for her. This seemed like more of a possibility now since Clifford was the ranch manager. If they kept him on in the same role, he could handle some of the things to give her more time to spread her focus.

"Are you planning to tell your mother that we'll be a little over two hours from her?"

"Do I have to?" she grumbled and looked up from the notebook where she had been working on a business plan for the last several hours.

"I think so." He sat one of the income logs aside and adjusted on the bed so he could look at her. "She's going to press as to why you didn't visit her today. It would be best to just come out and tell her that we're purchasing the ranch."

"Before then, I want to work out the details with you. Then I'll tell her and I'll make sure Colin is there too because I have a few choice words for him about his deceitful plan." She leaned back in the chair and watched him. "I received the official word that they will make exceptions due to the circumstances and I can take my final exams when we return. I'll graduate as planned."

"I figured they'd allow for it."

"I love the ranch and I'm so grateful for what you've done." She paused because she wasn't sure how to phrase what was running through her mind.

"I hear *but* coming."

"I have an idea on how to make two of my loves come together as one and to continue work like I do at the hospital."

"That would be?"

She pushed back from the table and went to sit next to him on the bed. "Mr. Cline downsized some of what he was doing since his wife got sick. There are still the stables for boarding, horse training, the riding lesson areas, and the important parts. But that other large building on the far side used to be additional living quarters. The rooms upstairs were small suites sometimes used for out of town guests. As you saw, the structure is still there but could use some work. I have the perfect idea for it."

"Well, do tell," he pressed when she paused.

"I want to set up a wellness retreat. I'll do physical therapy and Heather's a psychotherapist. I'd like to bring her on. You have taken great strides in the last several months, even spending time with some injured military personnel. You could offer great support for an amputee who came to the program. I think the three of us could make it a success."

"How does this tie into the ranch?"

"Neither one of us are going to put Clifford out of work. Which means a good majority of running the ranch won't be our daily responsibility." She was still working through all the thoughts that were jumbled up in her mind but it seemed like her plan could work. "This is what I went to school for and, while I always had the end game of owning the ranch, I thought I'd use my degree before owning this place. Now I see I can do both. The land surrounding the ranch is beautiful, amazing views, and trails that could be explored. It could be a place of feeling. With the three of us, we can do things the hospitals can't."

"What about a doctor? Medical staff? Those are important aspects as well."

"There's a doctor in town and maybe we can work something out with him that he'd come to the ranch. I just started outlining a business plan but, what do you think?"

"What you're putting together here is something that will be a great benefit to people like me when they come back from overseas."

"What *we're* doing," she corrected. "You really think I can get military service members to come to the ranch."

"Why not? Horses are great therapy animals, only beat out by dogs. This ranch will be beneficial to everyone. With the PT on site, you can do physical injuries, and with Heather, you open yourself up to more by being able to treat those with PTSD and other combat trauma."

"Then I want it to be veteran focused in honor of you, my dad, Weber, and all of those who didn't make it home."

"Not me but for the others. I'm no hero."

"You're my hero." She scooted closer and kissed him, not just to stop his protests but also because she wanted to. "We'll keep it small and intimate. Make it more about a place of healing than about being an amputee, or even needing PT. What do you think? Am I just dreaming?"

"I think what you want to do is ambitious, and if anyone can do it, I know you can." He took her hand and pulled her up next to him. "I was looking over this log book and it seems as though breeding should be something that is brought back to the ranch as well. There are still good breeding horses there. We discussed that briefly on the drive back."

"Breeding would be good for the ranch. I know there are some horses there but we'll have to purchase additional ones if it's something we're seriously considering. To bring that back like it was when Dad was alive, we'll need more than what Mr. Cline has now. He sold his best breeding mare."

"We can do that. The question is, can we handle both? If not, which one first?" He held her close to him, his fingers teasing down her bare arm. "I'd say breeding because even though we'd have to add to the stock, it would start bringing income in right away. We'll need to work on the buildings, add your PT area, and things like that. It's going to take a little time to get it up and running."

"Then let's start breeding immediately and work on the area. We'll make them both work but at first, we'll be a little more focused on the breeding aspect. Should I start looking for another breeding mare?"

"I'd offer but I don't know much about that. You and Clifford will have to teach me."

"Don't worry." She wriggled her head against his chest trying to find the perfect spot. "I still can't believe this. It's like a dream."

"I know what you mean." He pressed his cheek against the top of her head. "I keep waiting to wake up and find you gone. That you finally realized you can do better."

"I've got all I want with you." She let her heavy eyelids drift shut and just enjoyed the moment. Hers was a perfect and true admission. It didn't matter that he bought the ranch; he was everything she wanted. Getting the ranch represented just an added benefit.

If she had to choose between her dream of owning the ranch and being with him, she'd have chosen him hands down. She wanted to spend the rest of her life with this man, to wake up every morning in his embrace and to feel his warm lips against hers. This was living.

Staci sat by her mother's bedside, waiting for the right moment. It had been two days since they went to Kentucky. Two days of her mother's constant nagging to know the reason why Staci hadn't been at the hospital that day. Now she was ready to tell her; all she needed was for Colin to return from his dinner break. She'd tell them both at once and after she got it off her chest, she'd slip away with Kyle and they'd go for a late dinner. They wouldn't return to the hospital until late the next day. She needed time to recuperate after the fight she was undoubtedly about to have with her mother.

"I don't know why you come and visit me if you won't even tell me where you disappeared to."

"Mom…" She let out a deep sigh. "I don't see how the two are interchangeable. I'm here because you're my mother and you're in the hospital. I love you and want to see you better."

"Well you won't have to worry about that any longer. The doctors said as long as I can keep solid food down I can go home tomorrow. So your obligations will be over. You and *he* can go back to doing whatever it is you did the other day."

She had grown tired of how her mother had referred to Kyle and how she would say his name with such disgust. She had said so over the last few days but he had told her to just leave it be. It wasn't something to get all upset about. To him, the way she thought less of him was just another example of how much his life had changed since he had returned from overseas. She wanted to address this, but her mother had always been set in her ways. Instead of fighting with both of them, she had taken to showing him just how much he meant to her.

He gave her shoulder a gentle squeeze, as if reminding her it was fine. That no matter what comments her mother made about him, he wasn't going anywhere. They had more than a business arrangement. She loved him.

Before she decided what to say to her, Colin strolled back into the room carrying a dozen roses. The baby's breath made the red roses stand out in a sharp contrast. Since she had set things straight with Colin, he had taken to bringing her flowers every day. The hospital room was beginning to look like a florist. Did he think he'd win her mother over with flowers? That it was the way to make her agree to marry him?

She shoved those thoughts away. It wasn't her battle and she had enough to be concerned with. Now that he was back, the time had come to tell them about the ranch. Wanting reassurance, she reached up and laid her hand on Kyle's.

"Mom…"

"Just go. I can't even stand to see you sitting there acting like you care, when I know you're just counting down the minutes until you can get out of here and back to the hotel with him." She took the flowers Colin held out and brought them to her nose. "They smell beautiful. Thank you, darling."

"If I'm counting down the minutes until I can get away from you it's because of your attitude. The way you treat both of us. Kyle has done nothing to you; he's accompanied me because he cares about me. It's why he stands here and says nothing when you sit there and degrade him. Well, I'm tired of it. You might have treated me like this all my life but I won't stand by while you do it to him."

"Staci, it's okay."

She stood so she could look at him. "No, it isn't."

"I won't have you upsetting…"

She spun toward Colin, stopping him midsentence, and for a brief moment, she wondered what he saw in her eyes that made him step back. For the first time since the fight with her mother over her college major, she'd reached her boiling point. A person could only take so much before they stopped sitting there and allowing someone to continue to nitpick at them. Well, that time had finally arrived. It might have taken longer than normal but she'd had enough of the disrespectful comments directed at Kyle.

"Don't worry, Colin. I've only one thing to say and then we're leaving." She stepped back into Kyle's embrace and kept them both in view.

"Young lady, after that outburst, I think you better go back to your hotel room and remember what I taught you as a child. You treat your elders with respect. Until you can respect me and Colin, you're not welcome here."

"You were so anxious to know where we went the other day, coming up with all those scandalous tales of what we could have been up to. Now you want me to leave, fine." She snatched her bag from beside the chair and slipped it over her shoulder, completely aware of what she was doing. Her mother wouldn't let her just stroll from the hospital room, when she was finally ready to dish the truth, but it would have taught her a lesson if they simply walked out on her.

"Tell me." The hospital bed creaked up until her mother was sitting a little higher. "You've kept your secret for days. Now tell me."

"Sure, but when we return I expect you to treat Kyle with that same respect you were just demanding. The nasty comments about his burns or his injures are over. He got them while fighting for his country, a job he volunteered for to keep us all safe. He has asked me not to create waves and just ignore the nasty remarks but no longer. You can say what you want about me, but you will leave him out of this. He deserves your respect. Maybe you should remember that little thing you taught me. If you have nothing nice to say, then don't say anything at all."

"Fine." She practically spit out the word as if it left a nasty taste in her mouth.

"We went to see Mr. Cline." She tipped her head back to look at Kyle and smiled. "You are now looking at the soon-to-be proud owners of the ranch. We close on it in a few weeks."

"Impossible. We made sure he was selling it to someone else. I want better for my daughter than that ranch."

She took a deep breath as her suspicions that her mother played a part in Colin's actions were confirmed. *What an underhanded, nasty...* "Oh, mother dearest, I know you and Colin did your best to talk Mr. Cline into selling without informing me but it didn't work."

"I've worked to make a better life for you. To get you away from the ranch."

"Your dreams, not mine." She slipped her arm around Kyle's waist. "It's time I start living mine."

"What about your degree?"

"I'll take my last exams when we go home. We'll pack and come back to *our* ranch."

"There will be some changes made to the place." Kyle rubbed his hand down her arm. "Besides it being a working ranch, we're going to offer more. Staci's going to be able to combine her degree and her love for the ranch."

"How are you going to do that?" Colin pulled out the chair on the other side of the bed, sat down, and took her mother's hand into his.

"We're going to have a healing retreat. There's a lot of land and we're going to put it to good use. Heather has agreed to come and work for us once we have things up and running. She's going to be an in-house therapist. I'll be able to do physical therapy."

"Who's going to run the ranch?" Colin's dislike thickened his voice. "Horses need a lot of care and taking care of a ranch that size takes work."

"Clifford is the ranch manager and his son the lead horse trainer," she answered.

"I'll be heading up that part with them working directly with me," Kyle added.

"A naive child and an invalid running a ranch. Who'd have thought?" Her mother shook her head. "Mr. Cline's legacy will go down the drain within a year."

"That's enough!" Her voice rose as she fought back the tears and anger rising within. "We're leaving tomorrow, and I won't be stopping back before we go to the airport. You can give me a call when you've changed your attitude.

You'll know where to find me."

"Mrs. Pence." Even as she turned toward the door, Kyle stayed where he was. "You have an amazing daughter, and since we've been here I've realized she must take after her father because unlike you, there's not an evil bone in her body. She's compassionate, thoughtful, strong, and she'll fight for what she wants and believes in. Even though she's doing fine without your approval, there's no doubt in my mind she'd like it. Yet every chance she gives you, you push her further away. You lie to others, using her as your scapegoat, and still she puts up with it because she loves you. Don't take that love for granted."

"What do you know about it?" she snapped.

"I know one day you might wake up and your whole world would have turned upside down. There might be a day when she's not willing to stand by and let this continue. She's got more backbone than any woman I've ever known." He glanced at Staci before turning back to the bed. "Don't waste your chance."

"Maybe you should take your own advice because I think my daughter deserves better than you. She deserves not to have some broken down Marine with more scars than just those on the surface. I've lived through what your kind comes back with. I know the fear that boils within your loved ones at the possibility you might hurt them in a flashback rage." She glared at him a moment longer before turning her attention to Staci. "I'd have thought after the hell your father put us through you'd stay away from them. I knew you were volunteering at that military hospital, but I never believed you'd stoop so low as to be engaged to one."

"I love him and I don't have any fear when it comes to him. He'd never hurt me." She laced her fingers through his.

"I thought that same thing about your father once..." Her words trailed off. "Don't be so sure."

"He's not Dad." She tipped her head to the door. "Goodbye, *Mother*."

As they made their way out of the hospital, she couldn't help but feel that things between her and her mother would never be the same again. Sadness filled her as the door closed but she hoped it would lead to a better relationship with her mother in the future. Though somehow, she doubted it.

Chapter Twelve

Rather than going out for a quiet dinner to celebrate, they opted for takeaway Chinese and a movie back at the hotel. This had been Kyle's idea because after leaving the hospital, he knew she wasn't in the mood for what they had planned. They could reschedule the date until after the papers were final and the ranch was theirs. While Mrs. Pence had said some rude things, it was the look of sadness in Staci's eyes that hurt him the most. Tonight, he had plans to take that look out of her eyes. Tonight was about them and her mother's attitude wouldn't spoil it.

Staci curled against his body so he could wrap his good arm around her and he wondered how he could have gotten so lucky. Everything he'd said at the hospital was the truth, but what she meant to him was so much more than that. She was amazing and her level of caring was unmatched. She had given him a reason to live again and showed him he was still a man. The love he had for her couldn't be expressed in words.

"Kyle." Her fingers teased over each of the buttons on his shirt as she made her way up his chest.

"Don't, sugar. It's okay."

"No, it's not." She tipped her head up toward him. "The things she said—"

"Are her opinions and everyone's entitled to one. It doesn't change anything between us and she hasn't been the first one who has said those things to me. When military men and women return home injured or scared, so many want to push them back into a deep dark corner and forget about them. Some won't let that happen, while others become recluses and let the opinions of others force them into hiding." He squeezed her tighter to him. "Every once in a while, someone like you comes along to show a lonely Marine like me there's something worth living for. I love you, Staci, and nothing she says is going to change that. There's no need to apologize for her."

"I just feel bad. You know I don't feel that way, right? I love you for who you are not because I've taken pity on you. Pity has no place in our relationship. Your injuries brought us together since I was volunteering at the hospital, but they don't define us. You know that, right?"

"I do." He closed the distance between them and claimed her lips. The spiciness from the Chinese they'd had earlier still clung to her mouth, adding to the heat he felt raging within him. He tugged her bottom lip between his teeth and sucked it, before reclaiming her lips. When the kiss finally ended, she was breathless and her body pressed tightly against his. "Damn it, Staci. I want you."

"I thought you'd never say that." She smirked and let her fingers go to work on the buttons of his shirt.

"What?" He wasn't sure how he was supposed to take that or maybe it was the desire pouring through him that confused him.

"I've wanted you for weeks now. Being here in the same hotel room as you, so close to you…it's taken everything I've had not to push. I tried to give you the time I figured you needed but now your time's up."

"Communication." He nuzzled the curve of her neck and placed soft kisses along her collarbone.

"Huh?"

"I've been doing the same but for a different reason." He leaned back so he could look at her. "Your mother is right about one thing…"

"Let's not do that again." She slipped on top of him, straddling his waist. "You're the man I want. Now you've tied yourself to me as business partners, but I'm such a demanding woman I want more than just that. I want all of you."

"Sugar, you're shortchanging yourself. Look at me, I'm only half the man I was before."

"That's where you're wrong. Your injuries and scars don't make you less of a person. They show that you have strength and courage. Where others might have given up, you fought. When I stepped into that hospital room, I wasn't sure what I was going to find. I only knew Brenda thought you needed someone and I was supposed to be that person. When I left, I was worried I had done more damage than good. It wasn't until I showed up at your hotel room after you called and hung up that I realized how much you wanted to make a life for yourself. Before then, I don't think you had even decided if you wanted to live or die yet."

"Leaving the hospital, I thought I had. If you remember, I had the sidearm and whiskey in my bedside table. But I couldn't get this woman out of my thoughts." He grinned at her.

"Hmmm." She ran her hands up his sides. "She must have been something special."

"Oh, sugar, she is. Those whiskey brown eyes are so much better than real whiskey, and her attitude is not something to trifle with. But that's what I love about her." He reached up and tangled his hand in her hair, drawing her closer to him.

"Well then, I think it's time we show each other." She set to work on the last button of his shirt.

"Or scare you off," he tried to tease but wasn't able to keep the uncertain edge out of his voice. He stopped the dread from welling inside him at the thought of her seeing him naked. He kept in shape, working out more now than he did before his injures in order to keep the strength in his remaining limbs, but that wasn't his issue. The problem was the scars hiding under his clothes. She had accepted his lack of limbs and the scars she could see—those were the flaws he couldn't deny—but these were nothing like what he had hidden under the shirt.

"I'm not going anywhere."

"You might change your mind when you see the horrors under my shirt." Even he didn't like to look. He'd dash past the mirrors after a shower so he wouldn't have to look at them. He'd throw on a shirt, hiding them from view, and then he'd continue to get dressed.

"Words won't convince you, so let me show you." She slipped the last button through the opening and took hold of his shirt. "Nothing can change what I feel for you. Not superficial scars, not my mother's attitude, nothing."

She kept her gaze locked on his as she slid the shirt open. His breath caught in his throat as if the simple movement of taking a breath would break the moment and send her running away from him in horror. He knew this moment would come eventually but had wanted to push it off as long as he could. The scars from the flames were something he didn't want or have to face, and pretend they weren't there.

She glanced down at his chest and slid her hands over his unmarred flesh before slowly moving toward the burns. The worst of them sat on his chest and he remembered the flames licking his body just before he'd lost consciousness. His last thought had been that he was going up like a barbeque and there had been nothing he could do about it.

"Stay with me." She wiggled her hips, grinding herself gently against the front of him.

He shoved those memories away and focused on the woman before him.

The woman he was afraid he was about to lose.

He wanted to curse the day he signed up for the Marines, but he didn't because that would mean he would never have met her. Better to have her for a brief period than to have never known her kindness and her touch.

She slid her fingers over the first of the scars—just a soft pucker of the skin, but as she moved her fingers farther along, she'd find the deformed, hard, textured ones that crawled half way across his chest. Even as she found the worst of the burns, her fingers explored the contours of each terrible wound.

"See, nothing has changed." She scooted lower, positioning her hips near his mid-thigh, and lowered her head toward his chest. She started at his bellybutton, kissing her way up his chest, her hands on his sides while her nails dragged lightly across the skin. She worked her way over where the worst of the burns began and ran her tongue along them.

The intimacy of her touches, the way she worked so hard to show him the scars didn't matter, moved him deeply, slammed home into his chest—his heart. Maybe it didn't matter what the shell looked like but what resided inside a person's heart. He wasn't sure he completely believed that before, but if she could love him even with his scars and missing body parts, then maybe it was possible for others to find a love like he had.

Need and desire tore at him. He grabbed hold of her sweater and slid it along her torso. "I need you…now." The words came out more of a growl than he had planned.

"I'm not done." She tipped her head up just enough to look at him as she kissed a rather nasty scar that puckered up and off his chest.

"Another time." He wanted her naked and his shaft buried deep inside her. Knowing she could accept the scars he'd been trying to hide from her and everyone else, he couldn't restrain himself any longer. The wait was over.

"Seems like I'm on top so I control the speed." She leaned up and tugged her shirt off the rest of the way before reaching behind her and unclasping her bra. "Maybe I should draw this out longer." She rubbed a hand along the crotch of his jeans, meeting his hard shaft straining to be released.

"Don't think I won't roll you over and have my way with you."

"Just try it and see how far that gets you." Through his jeans, she grasped his shaft. "Women hold all the power in sex. A few simple words can stop all the fun: *Not now, honey, I have a headache.*"

"Sugar." He reached up and took one of her nipples between his fingers, gently squeezing. "You want this as much as I do."

"It would seem as if your need is worse." She unbuttoned his jeans and tugged down the zipper. "It's like opening a present on Christmas morning; the excitement is just the same."

"I've never been good at waiting. I want you naked now."

"You have more clothes on than I do." She pulled his shaft from the thin material of his boxers. "I'd say we should rectify that but I just found the best part."

"It will be there but I can't access your sweet spot with these pants on. So up and take them off."

With a huff, she lifted herself off him and took them off. As she did, he tugged off his jeans and boxers, completely revealing his prosthetic leg, but she had seen that part of him before. Sharing a hotel room meant he couldn't hide that as he put it on and took it off. He went to take off his shirt when her hands reached over and slipped it down his shoulders, letting it pool behind him.

With both of them naked, he couldn't keep his desire in check any longer. He wrapped his good arm around her and pulled her against his body, then, his mouth claimed her as the desire exploded within. He never thought he'd have a chance with a woman again and now that he had her with him like this, he wasn't going to waste a second of it. He pushed his tongue into her mouth, exploring, and gently gliding over her teeth. She nipped at his bottom lip as he pulled back.

"I want you on top of me."

"Maybe I wanted to do it doggie style," she teased as she slipped back on top of him. "It's been years since I've been on a stallion; let's see if I remember this."

"I have no doubt it will all come back to you." He reached between her legs, slipping his finger between her folds to make sure she was ready for him. He was met with warmth and wetness. A soft moan escaped from her as his finger caressed over her clit.

"If you do that too long, I'm not going to make it. It's been a while…"

He sped his pace and she arched her back, tipping her head back. "Please, Kyle, I want you inside me…now." The last part came out on the tip of a moan.

He wanted to watch her squirm above him until she found the release her body so badly needed, but she was right—he wanted to be inside of her. He wanted to feel her muscles constrict around his shaft as she orgasmed. "Lift up."

She did as he asked and he adjusted so his shaft was just below her entry. "Slowly." He guided himself into her as she lowered herself down. He had barely slid past her entrance when she let out a moan and her pace changed. She nearly slammed herself down onto him. The need had her propelling herself up and down while he met her with a thrust of his own.

He kept his hand on her hip as they matched thrust for thrust. With each stroke, the fire within him burned brighter and hotter. His climax loomed in the distance but he wanted to see her release before he would allow himself the pleasure. He wanted to see her eyes gloss over and the utter joy as she climaxed around his shaft.

For a brief moment, he wished he still had both of his arms so he could wrap them around her, but when she grabbed hold of his biceps, he forgot about it. She had been the only one, besides the medical staff, who had touched his injured arm. The intimacy of her touch nearly busted his control. He arched his hips into her a little harder than the last time.

"Kyle!" she cried, her voice tight and full of need.

"Come on, sugar…" His fingers tightened onto her hip, speeding her pace up and down.

"Don't stop." She held onto him for all it was worth, riding his thrusts like a bull rider. She leaned forward, her breast jiggling with each movement, just out of reach of his mouth, taunting him. She closed her eyes as her body tightened around him. She was nearly there.

"Look at me," he demanded.

She opened her eyes but it wasn't like she was truly seeing him. A glaze within their depths suggested she wasn't completely there, but feeling the effects of her oncoming climax. "Faster, Kyle…please…"

She slammed down into him as he arched up to meet her, driving the force of each pump. He thrust deeper and faster into a perfect rhythm.

"Oh, Kyle!" she moaned as she slammed down onto him again.

Her muscles squeezed tight around him, the final act he needed to find his own release. Breathless, she leaned forward, her body pressed again his chest, while he stayed buried deep within her. Needing to see her, he brushed her hair from her face. As if understanding what he wanted, she tipped her head to look up at him, her eyes glossy and dreamy—the aftermath of amazing sex.

"That was worth the wait." She slid off him and curled against his body.

"Wait until round two, sugar." Contentment filled him as he pulled the blanket over them. He cradled her, caressing her spine with long, lazy strokes. Everything had come together and brought him the woman he could have only dreamed about. He nuzzled the top of her head. "You make me whole, Staci Pence. I love you."

PART THREE

Chapter Thirteen

It had been a few months since Kyle had married Staci, but he couldn't get enough of her. He stood on the porch of their home, overlooking United Homefront Ranch, and there in the distance he could see her teaching one of the local children how to ride. They had expanded the ranch in so many ways, but the riding school had been Clifford's idea. The school was something that everyone agreed would give back to the community and would keep the legacy of the Clines alive since they had done the school each summer. Normally, Clifford and his son ran the school, but today, they had gone to Nashville to pick up their new mare. Staci had covered the afternoon class while Kyle had dealt with some of the business details that needed to be attended to.

When he'd purchased the place, he wasn't sure what he was even doing; he only knew he couldn't let it slip through Staci's fingers again. She loved this place and after everything she had done for him, it seemed to be the best way to repay her. Little did he know that he'd actually find something he truly enjoyed, a calling he thought he wouldn't find since his military career had been tugged away from him. He loved the ranch and everything it was becoming.

The retreat section of the ranch had just been finished. Heather would move into a small cabin on the grounds in just under two weeks, and their first client would arrive at the end of the month. Everything Staci had wanted had come together. It couldn't have been better if he had arranged it all himself. Sometimes things just fell into place.

There was just one other thing he wanted, and if things went the way he had hoped, there'd be a call coming in soon with the news. Until then, he'd have to find other ways of busying himself. Instead of going to his wife and having his way with her like he wanted, he took another swig of his beer and waited. She'd be done soon enough with the class and then the two of them had the evening free. They'd take advantage of it because after the retreat opened, things could get a little hectic.

"Mr. Phillips." Josefina pushed open the screen door and stepped out onto the porch. "Sir, there's a call for you. He says it's urgent."

"Thank you." He took the phone and wondered how he went from being a foster kid to having a ranch and a housekeeper. Josefina had been the housekeeper at the ranch for years under Mr. and Mrs. Cline, and when they sold, she had stayed on. Her husband worked in the stable and they too had a little cabin on the property. *Guess I don't just have a stable of horses, but also of friends.* He smirked and brought the phone to his ear. "Phillips here."

"Lance Corporal Phillips, it's Sergeant Major Graves. I've got good news."

This was the call he had been waiting for, but the excitement that had flooded his veins only minutes before was gone, leaving him deflated. The voice of the Sergeant Major had only sent memories of his Marine days flooding back. He hadn't had a lot of contact with Sergeant Major Graves, but it wasn't the man that brought the memories back to the forefront of his thoughts. It was everything this call meant.

Keep it together, you're doing this for Gunny.

The sun was setting over the ranch as Staci climbed the steps up to the house. Kyle sat in the porch swing, beer in hand, and a glass of iced tea sitting on the railing waiting for her. This was a perfect ending to a good day. She'd curl up against his body as the last rays of sun disappeared over the horizon.

"Hey sugar, how was the class?"

"Good." She took a long drink from the glass before sitting it back on the railing. "The Harrison boy was a handful as always, but his sister is a doll. I'll be glad when Clifford is back tomorrow."

"It will be nice to have him here for when your mare gives birth."

"My mare." She shook her head and sat down next to him. "Like you don't have a thing for sweet Abbie."

"She's the first horse you talked me into riding, so she might hold a special spot, but that's all you're getting from me. I still can't believe you got me on a horse."

"Abbie was good for you to start with but you're doing okay with Outlaw." She curled her legs up under her and leaned against his chest.

"Yeah the horse we have to basically tie to the barn to get him to stay here. He's just like his namesake, an outlaw. We're always having to take off and look for him."

"You know he's just going to the neighboring farm. He's got a thing for Hopscotch." She smirked thinking about their solid black stallion, Outlaw, with the beautiful caramel and gold mare from just up the road. The two of them were destined to be together. "If only we could get them to sell her to us, I don't think old Outlaw would ever leave our land."

"I'm working on him. But there's something else I need to talk to you about." She started to move away but he sat his beer aside and held her there. "I heard from Sergeant Major Graves today about the cook-off they're doing. Lucky was chosen and I need to go to Colorado to do a few interviews with him. Promotional appearances to give this the biggest bang and all that crap."

"When?"

"The day after tomorrow."

"Oh…" She tried to figure out what they'd do with Abbie. Their first mare was about to give birth and she wanted to be there for it but she also wanted to be with him. Clifford and the other ranch hands could handle Abbie but she felt the birthing was her responsibility.

"I know, sugar. The timing is bad with Abbie and all, but we knew this was a possibility if he was chosen. I need to go, make amends…I need my Gunny to know I don't blame him for what happened. I haven't seen him since I was in the hospital and I treated him like shit. This is not just for him but for myself. To close the door on my past once and for all."

"I'll make arrangements for Abbie. It will be fine."

"No, I want you to stay here. Abbie needs you more. She's more comfortable with you than anyone else and in her state, she needs that. I'll only be gone a few days." He cupped the side of her face. "I know you want to go with me but I'll be fine."

"You're going to have to relive those horrors. To hash them out in front of reporters."

"I know sugar, but everything that happened brought me here to you. That's what counts. *Us.* Our love and our ranch."

She slipped her hand around his waist. "Are you sure? Abbie will be fine. Clifford will see to it and if I had to I'd call my mother." She hated the very thought of doing it but she would if it meant she could be with him.

"There's no way I'm going to be the reason for that fight." He kissed her forehead. "I'll be fine."

"My mother would have her usual comments but you know she wouldn't let anything happen to Abbie. She's a vet and that's more important to her than, well, anything…me included." She hated that it sounded like she was jealous of the animals. After her father's death, all she wanted was her mother's approval.

114

She never got it and now she didn't care if she ever did.

"True, but every time you two get together you fight. You can't even talk on the phone without having to defend me and for that, I'm sorry."

"It's not you. It has always been like this. Mom always found fault in everything I did. I'm sorry that she has taken you as her newest target." She untucked her legs so she could turn to look at him better. "You didn't ask for any of this; you were just kind of dragged into it because of me. You don't deserve the way she treats you."

"I told you before I let it wash over me. Nothing's going to change her attitude unless she wants to change. What's important is that we're happy." He slipped his hand under her shirt. "Now I think there are better ways to spend the evening than talking about Mrs. Pence."

"I second that." She rose from the swing and held out her hand. They'd make their way inside and enjoy each other. Maybe the memories they made that night would help get him through the time in Colorado, when he'd be reliving the hell he had gone through to come to her.

Chapter Fourteen

Kyle stood in front of the address that Sergeant Major Graves gave him and tried to gather the courage to go to the door. It had been more than a year since he'd seen Gunnery Sergeant Lucky Diamond. Now he was about to show up out of the blue. A letter from his former foster mother had alerted him to the cooking competition that was pinning the different branches against each other to raise money for wounded veterans. The letter had come as a surprise since their last communication had been during his deployment. But now he knew it was all part of some master plan to give him a chance to do something for Lucky and give to other Marines who came back injured as he had.

He took a deep breath, headed up the walkway, and rang the doorbell. He stood there waiting; with each second his unease grew and he wished Staci were standing next to him. *You'll be back home with her soon enough.*

The door opened to reveal a woman in a brown with white polka dot dress. Her mouth dropped open when she saw him. He looked down to make sure he had put on his prosthetic arm, which he had, so that hadn't shocked her, and in the darkness there was no way she could have seen the full extent of the burns.

"Private First Class Phillips." The words came out in a breathless gasp.

"It's Lance Corporal now, but it would seem that you have one up on me.

I'm looking for Gunnery Sergeant Diamond."

"I'm Madison North." She held out a hand to him and as he took it, he noticed she had given him the one he could use his good arm to shake. "His um…handler."

"Isn't he the lucky one?" he teased before growing serious. "I'm taking it from your surprise neither of you were aware I was coming."

"I'm sorry but no. Was this planned?"

He nodded. "I received confirmation the other day from Sergeant Major Graves. Maybe I should come back."

"No, come in."

"I think it would be best if you told him I was here first." He nodded to the bench on the porch. "I'll just wait here and if he wants to see me he can come out. If not…"

She nodded. "Give me a second. I know he'll want to see you."

He didn't bother to sit down, but instead stood near the edge of the porch, looking up at the night sky. The stars didn't seem as bright here; too many lights interfered and hid them from view, while out on the ranch there was nothing but darkness, allowing him to see all the stars in the sky. He had always lived in the city before but now he wasn't sure he could ever leave the country. He was becoming a country man, even completed the look with the dusty cowboy boots and hat. *What have you turned me into, Staci?*

He tried to focus on the sky to keep the memories at bay but it wasn't working. They were seeping in, threatening to take him over. He didn't want to relive the memory of the mission that stole his limbs and left him injured. A smirk pulled up the corners of his lips. A year ago, he'd have called himself a cripple, but now he didn't see himself as that any longer. He was injured but Staci had proven to him over and over he wasn't less of a man now.

A car pulled out of the driveway across the street and backfired. That was all that was needed to send the memories flooding forward.

They had been following a lead that should have led them straight to one of the terrorists they had been searching for. With each mile, his unease worsened. He knew he was picking up on his Gunny's nerves as he scanned the surroundings from the passenger seat of the lead vehicle. Gunnery Sergeant Diamond had been about to say something when gunfire broke out in nearly every direction, leaving no place to take cover. He had been unable to do anything but wait until they found cover. His best friend, Private First Class Weber, was returning fire from the turret but the insurgent numbers were too great. Surrounded…they were going to die.

"Gunny?" Corporal Juan Torres, the Humvee driver, nodded toward the roadblock before them.

"Fuck!" Gunny hollered to Torres but Kyle had barely heard it over the gunfire. "Reverse. Fall back. Now!"

Torres slammed the Humvee into reverse and plowed backward. On the radio, Gunny ordered the two additional Humvees to fall back. Blood dripped down from the turret. Weber was hit.

Without thinking Kyle knew he had to do something for his friend. He tugged off his seat belt and tried to access Weber's injuries. He wasn't a corpsman but he might be able to put pressure on the wound until they could get to safety and Doc, their corpsman, could get to them from the second Humvee. Even injured, Weber was firing, making each shot count, but there was too much blood. Weber wasn't going to last long up there.

"Weber!" He hollered but got no response.

"Swing left and turn us around," Gunny ordered as they neared a clearing without anyone blocking the way. They were nearly there. Just a little farther and they'd be out of range. Above him, the machine gun fire stopped and Phillips helped the now unconscious Weber back into the Humvee.

With a hard left, Torres had them facing the right way. Kyle got into position, taking over the turret. In the distance, the other two Humvees had managed to turn around as well. They were dealing with less incoming gunfire and were holding their own. It wasn't his worry; he had to focus on returning fire on the insurgents who were still a threat. It was now his job to defend their Humvee while Gunny and Torres got them out of there. One moment the noise was deafening and the next, the assault subsided, only his machine gun continued. Even though they were no longer shooting at them, he couldn't stop himself from firing. If he stopped, they would begin again.

Torres was nearing the road again after their off road adventure to get turned around. Scanning the perimeter, he had a brief moment to realize that every insurgent that had been there had moved back. Something wasn't right.

He had barely had time to register the change in their surroundings when an IED exploded, sending their Humvee skyward. As they were tossed through the air, he didn't have time to get inside.

Each second seemed like minutes as they were tossed around in the Humvee before it finally landed on its side. He flew through the air, and pain exploded throughout his body. So much that he wasn't sure what hurt the most. The heat…flames. They were everywhere.

He landed hard, his Gunny's voice in the distance hollering for him, gunfire even farther. It all seemed to be overcast as he fought to keep conscious.

He shoved his memories away as the door behind him opened and he turned to find Gunnery Sergeant Diamond standing there. The surprise was clear in his eyes but a friendly smile etched up the corners of his lips.

"Shocked that I'm here?" he asked and when Lucky didn't say anything, he proceeded. "The last time I saw you, I was ready to give up. I didn't see any reason for living. Not when I was down to one arm and one leg. I was half the man I was, but that all changed."

"I can't believe it." Lucky stepped back. "Come in."

"Well, believe it. I'm alive because of you. Your parting words had me so angry that they called in someone to speak with me."

Lucky shut the door before turning back to Kyle. "I'm not sure why I'm to credit for you being alive."

"Because four months ago, I married her. She came into my life to ease the anger, guilt, and regret. She showed me I was still a man and she fell in love with me. If it wasn't for you turning my self-pity into anger, I'd have never met her and wouldn't be here."

"Here…as in Colorado, and doing this competition?" Lucky let out a deep laugh and shook his head. "Damn, I should have kept my mouth shut and let you kill yourself."

"Gunny, there are plenty of Marines who could use the ten thousand you could win for them, and there's no one better to do this than you." He waited until they were in the living room and had taken seats, before adding, "I nominated you for this not as some payback, but because we need someone like you fighting for us."

"I cooked for you guys because I enjoyed it. I never wanted any recognition for it."

He nodded and leaned back on the sofa. "I've learned sometimes we don't get what we want, but in the end it turns out better than you expected." For him, it had brought him Staci; for Lucky, he wasn't sure what it would bring him but there was no doubt in Kyle's mind it would turn out for the best for him as well.

They spent the next hour talking, all the while avoiding the subject of their last mission together, even though the shadow of it lingered just beneath the surface. They were both remembering the events of that day, but neither of them wanted to say anything. Instead, they talked about the competition, Staci, and even the Colorado Mountains. Finally, unable to take it any longer he leaned forward and said, "You know I don't blame you, right?"

"It was my responsibility to see that you all made it home. You and Weber were PFC's on your first deployment and look what I let happen. You might not blame me but don't doubt that I blame myself every day. Weber and your blood is on my hands. Widow Weber's grief is on my conscience, just as much as the fact that Weber will never see his son grow up."

"We all knew the dangers when we volunteered, that we might not make it back and if we did, we might not do so whole. That didn't stop any of us. It isn't your fault. The blood that was shed that day should be on the hands of those who placed the IED, not yours." Even as the words left his mouth, he knew Lucky would have to come to terms with the guilt when he was ready. It wouldn't be something anyone else could do for him.

Just as Kyle had done. It had taken Staci coming into his life for him to accept how things turned out. Maybe, there was something happening between his Gunny and Madison. The brief few minutes he had seen her made him wonder if there wasn't more of a connection between them than just her being his handler.

"I don't like that they brought you into town to shoot some fucking interviews talking about that day. It's a disgrace…"

"Gunny…" He paused because he was about to step into uncharted territories contradicting his superior.

"Just out with it, Phillips, I'm not your Gunny any longer."

"That's where you're wrong." He smirked because for him, Lucky would always be someone he looked up to and admired. "But fine. They didn't bring me here to highlight the bullshit that happened, but because I'm the one that threw your name in for this. I contacted Sergeant Major Graves and he took it to the brass. There are Marines who are coming back all the time fucked up. They could use the money you could win them. But not only that, you'll be doing it in Weber's memory and for all the others who didn't make it back. We owe them this."

"For such a young shit you sure have life all figured out." Lucky leaned back against the sofa and eyed Kyle.

"If so, then it's because of what you taught me and what I've gone through. Though I better give my wife some credit as well or she'll have my head." Kyle chuckled. "After all this, I'd love for you to meet her. She's a spitfire and wouldn't let me give up."

"Sounds like a good woman. I know that type all too well. Seems like I've got one on my hands right now."

"Madison? So there is more than just the handler job." Now that the subject was started he wanted confirmation. During Kyle's time with the platoon, Lucky had had his share of women. There were always women willing to be seen with a Marine, so none of them had ever been without a date when they needed one. However, the Gunny had always seemed to compare them to someone else. Was this time different?

"Maddie…my handler." Lucky shook his head. "In more ways than one, I guess, and like yours, she's feisty."

"Good for you. There's nothing better than having a spitfire woman by your side."

Lucky sat there for a moment lost in thought before finally nodding. "I've been keeping tabs on you. Seems you went and bought a ranch for your woman. Now that sounds awfully familiar, as well. Years ago, I bought Maddie's childhood home, with the hopes that one day we'd live there with our own family. Though it never worked out."

"My sugar would say that it's never too late to get your happily ever after. Though I think sometimes they have to beat us over the head a few times for us to see what we really want." He grabbed his cowboy hat from where he'd sat it and rose. "It's been a long flight and I should get some sleep. We've got a busy few days with interviews lined up."

"Thanks for stopping by."

Kyle nodded. "I thought we should work through the unease of our last meeting without cameras around." He strolled toward the door before turning back to look at Lucky. "Forgive me if it's out of line, but it sounds like you let her slip through your fingers before. Don't make the same mistake again. I saw the look in her eyes when she opened the door and saw me. She knew seeing me would bring back memories she didn't want you to have to live through again. She's protective of you and cares about you. A woman like that is worth all the gold in the world."

Chapter Fifteen

The days in Colorado passed at the speed of a snail, while all Kyle wanted to do was get home to Kentucky to his wife and their ranch. Interview after interview had torn shreds from him. He was tired of reliving what had gotten them to that place. Now there was only one last stop before he could board his plane.

Up ahead he could see the iron gates of the cemetery. Glen Haven, Colorado had been more than an hour's drive but it was one thing he wasn't leaving Colorado without doing. He owed Weber that much. Paying his respects at the grave of his fallen brother wasn't enough but it was all he had to offer at the moment. If he had more time, he'd have made arrangements to visit Mrs. Weber. He hit the steering wheel of the rental car. "If guilt didn't tear through me at the thought of seeing her, I would."

Cassy Weber and her son, Johnny, had brought her husband home to bury him in the family cemetery. She wanted him there so he'd be close since she moved back to their hometown to raise her son. She had made something good come out of Weber's death but it didn't replace her husband or a father for her son. As he drove through the gates of the cemetery, the memory of the articles they had published on her and her new business popped into his thoughts.

Sewn with Love. A business brought about in memory of her husband where she turns the uniforms and clothes of fallen service members into something special for military spouses. This started out as a way to remember those who were killed in action, but it had gone far beyond that. Any spouse or family member could send in their clothes and she would turn them into whatever they wanted. Quilts were the biggest thing, but she also did pillows, purses, and more.

Cassy Weber has done something for his memory, and for the memories of others who have died during their service to our country. She's turning tragedy into something that's cherished. She gave her husband's life and his death meaning, and by doing that, she's giving others closure.

He shoved the car into park. One comment in the article he read last made him want to scream. *Cassy Weber's destiny was brought to life because of her husband's death.* Her destiny? How could anyone's destiny be to lose the person they loved in order to make crafts? Weber's life meant more to him, and sure meant more to her, than that. Right? Someday he'd find out the answer, but right then, he needed to focus on the closure he needed with Weber's death. Until then, he couldn't do anything to help Cassy. Even then, she might not want to see him.

If he had left Weber in the turret instead of changing places with him so he could return fire on the insurgents, then the man would be alive today to be with his wife and son. He might have been injured like Kyle but injured was better than dead.

At the gravestone, he ran his hand along the top. Flowers had been laid out before it. From the fresh footprints in the grass, it was clear someone had been there recently. Had Cassy paid a visit? How often did the widow come to her husband's grave? One article, nearly a year ago, mentioned that she came daily but he hated to think of her making visits every day to her husband's gravestone. To him, that wasn't getting over the loss, only prolonging the pain. How long was long enough to grieve?

He shook his head. "What do I know about grief like she's experiencing?

I've never lost a family member." Weber's death was the only one that counted to him and part of that was because he blamed himself for it. Getting up in the turret might have been what saved his life, but it left Weber to die.

"Excuse me," a soft voice called from behind him.

He turned to find the one woman he hoped not to see—Cassy Weber. She strolled toward him with her long brown hair flying in the wind. He wasn't sure why, but it surprised him she looked happy. No dark circles under her eyes, no tears, and there was even a smile on her face.

"Kyle…" A smile etched across her face as she came closer. The smile could only do so much to hide the shock in her eyes. Not all the surprise was from him being there; some of it was due no doubt to her seeing his injuries for the first time. "I can't believe it's you."

"I'm sorry I hadn't come before." He suddenly felt like a schoolboy who was late back from recess. "I couldn't…" He wasn't sure what he couldn't do. Couldn't come to the grave of his best friend? Couldn't meet the eyes of the widow he helped create? See the little boy that had been like a nephew to him and know that he was now fatherless?

She placed a bundle of fresh flowers at the foot of the headstone and wrapped her arms around Kyle. "Don't worry about that now. It's so good to see you."

"I should have come sooner." He stood there unable to do anything more than slip his one good arm around her. "I should have been at the funeral. I should have…" *saved him.*

"Nonsense. There was nothing you could have done. You were recovering from your own injuries." She stepped back. "While that excuses you up until you left the hospital. Since then I had expected to see you. Johnny has wondered where Uncle Kyle has been."

That sent a chill right through him. *Poor Johnny, too young to lose your daddy.* He and Weber had bonded so quickly during boot camp that he had spent a lot of time with the Weber family. Including holidays and weekly Sunday dinners when they weren't deployed. They had been the closest thing he had to family. Poor Johnny must have been confused losing his father, and it couldn't have been easier for the boy with Uncle Kyle suddenly gone as well. "I'm sorry." He knew it wasn't good enough but what else could he say? In truth he just couldn't face Cassy and Johnny after he let them down.

"Stop apologizing and come home with me. He'll be so excited to see you."

"I don't have much time. I'm flying back to Kentucky in a few hours, but if you don't mind, I'd like to stop by and see him."

"You know I don't. You're family." She reached forward and placed her hand on his arm. "I'm sorry, too."

"What for?" There was nothing she should be sorry for. He was the guilty party here, not her.

"I should have come to see you at the hospital…" Tears swam in her eyes and she glanced at the gravestone. "Losing him…it was just too much. I had to get away. My father passed away a few years ago, leaving me my childhood home. Without thinking about anyone else, I packed up what I could in the car and took off. I couldn't even go back to get our stuff, but thankfully our friends rallied together and everything arrived a few weeks later."

"You had to do what was best for you and Johnny. Trust me when I say that I wasn't in the best frame of mind then. A visit then wouldn't have done either of us any good, but we can make up for it now."

"This place is good for us. It's not like it was when he was alive but I'm making the best of things for Johnny's sake. My baby sister lives here so she's helping with Johnny, and there's other family."

He nodded. "It sounds like you're doing okay. I'd like to play a part in Johnny's life if you'll allow it. I mean maybe my injuries…"

"Uncle Kyle is always welcome. He loves you and misses you."

Relieved, he smiled. That little boy meant a lot to him and though he had distanced himself before he suddenly wanted to make up for lost time. "I'm married now and we have a ranch in Kentucky. Maybe you two would come for a visit. I'm sure he'd like the horses."

"As for the ranch I don't know…horses? He's such a little boy…" She stepped back and eyed him. "I didn't even notice until you mentioned the ranch. I guess I was so caught up in seeing you here, but you've changed. Look at you. Your wife has turned you into a cowboy."

"Surprising I know, but it suits me." He smirked. "I never thought I'd find something I enjoyed doing after the Marines, but it's kind of amazing. Staci, my wife, always dreamed of owning a ranch her father worked at. She got her dream and I got her. It all worked out. Plus, she's doing something amazing with the place. We opened a healing retreat there—United Homefront Ranch—focused on vets. She graduated with her physical therapy degree right around the time we bought the ranch, so she's doing that there. Her best friend Heather is a therapist so she's on staff as well."

"Sounds like you're doing your part to make the world better."

"Just like you." He nodded to her quilted bag made from Weber's old uniform. "I've been following what you've been doing. Sewn with Love. It's great."

"It's something small that maybe will bring closure to someone." She reached up and ran her hands over Weber's dog tags that she wore around her neck. His wedding band strung along the chain to lie next to the tags. "Sounds silly but when I put these on, they made me feel closer to him, and even now I can't bring myself to take them off. Johnny is so young but I found him curled up with one of his father's shirts. It's what gave me the idea. I turned a few of them into a blanket and to this day, Johnny is nearly inseparable from it. I never expected it to turn into a business, especially not like it is. I have more requests than I could have imagined. My sister put in her notice at her job to help. Even with the two of us, we have more than we can handle, but I can't turn people away. Not when I know how much that's helped Johnny."

"Have you thought about hiring someone else?"

"I have, but it needs to be the right person. Someone who cares about what we're doing as much as I do. Not someone who just needs a job." She dropped her grasp on the dog tags. "Come on, let's go see Johnny."

He glanced back to where his rental car was parked but there wasn't another vehicle to be seen. "Where's your car?"

"Actually, I walked, I just live through those woods. There's a small path. I'll ride with you to show you the way, so you don't have to trek back through to your car." She pressed her fingers to her lips, kissing them, before pressing them to the gravestone. "My love, I'll be back later."

"I can give you a few minutes."

She shook her head; her brown hair waved around until she brushed it back behind her shoulders again. "No, it's fine. It might sound crazy to you but I'll be back. I normally come over twice a day."

"Twice?" He did his best to keep the surprise out of his voice but he doubted he was able to completely, though if she caught it she ignored it.

"It's better than before. Actually, I'm not normally here at this time of day. I come early in the morning before Johnny gets up, but last night I was up late finishing a project and overslept. I had to wait until the housekeeper I've hired was back from running the shipments to the post office and grocery shopping. She's a blessing and helps to look after Johnny. She's like a grandmother to him."

He led the way to the rental car and realized that he had been dreading seeing Cassy because he thought she'd blame him as much as he blamed himself. Even if she didn't, it couldn't change the guilt he had. Weber was his best friend and he had played a role in getting him killed. He wasn't sure he'd ever be able to come to terms with that.

"Kyle…" She paused next to the passenger car door he held open for her.

"I need you to know…I don't blame you. Nothing that happened is your fault."

"Bullshit. If I hadn't changed places with him he'd still be here."

"No, Kyle." She placed her hand over his on the top of the door. "His injuries killed him, not the IED. He was dead when you pulled him inside."

Chapter Sixteen

It was late when Kyle arrived back at the ranch and he was exhausted. The interview schedule had taken more out of him than a full day of work on the ranch. It wasn't as physically draining but emotionally so—to relive the memories of his last missions was bad enough but to answer questions about them, his service, his recovery, and his life now proved worse. That mission and his military service was something he wanted to put behind him. He had finally gotten to the point that, when he looked in the mirror and saw his scars, or when he donned his prosthesis, he wasn't constantly reminded of that dreaded day. The interviews, though, brought it all back to the forefront of his memory, including his nightmares.

Even with that, he wouldn't have changed nominating Lucky for the cook-off. It gave his Gunny the recognition for his cooking skills that he deserved, and it was a way in which Kyle could give back to him. The competition was for a good cause too, a cause that was important to him, since everything he had gone through.

The trip had also reconnected him with Cassy and Johnny. Even hours after he had left them, Cassy's words kept playing through his thoughts. *He was dead before you pulled him in.* Was it true? He wasn't sure, but he'd find out. Lucky would know but he hadn't wanted to throw off the competition so he hadn't called. He'd see what he could find out on his own before he bothered his Gunny. It wouldn't bring Weber back, but he needed to know the truth. To make certain his action of bringing Weber into the Humvee hadn't been what led to his death. This would bring him closure.

Yet, closure would have to wait a little longer because there was something else he wanted more.

Staci.

He stepped inside his home and let his sea bag drop to the floor next to the front door. With a deep breath, he took in everything he missed. The sweet scent of apple pie Josefina must have cooked earlier that day, along with a roast that must have been dinner. He had never valued the sweet smell of home cooking until Josefina. She had a way in the kitchen that would send even the strongest man to his knees—which was great for him and Staci since neither of them had time to cook and his cooking skills were seriously lacking.

"I was waiting for you in bed," Staci's soft voice called as she strolled toward him in a nearly sheer baby doll nightgown. "Welcome home, husband."

She stood there with her hair cascading down around her shoulders. The thin material left nothing to the imagination, and all he could think about was how much he wanted her. "Oh, sweet sugar, I've missed you." He went to her, pressed her against the wall, and kissed her. His tongue dived between her lips as he slid his hand beneath the material and found her naked. Instantly, his shaft hardened, sending undeniable need pulsing through him.

Her hand slipped between them and rubbed against the front of his jeans, his hard shaft meeting her. "I'd say you missed me," she teased, when they broke the kiss. "Take me."

He didn't want to take the time to walk the length of the hall to their master bedroom. Instead, he slipped his zipper down, freeing his shaft from the confines of his pants. "Wrap your legs around my waist."

She did as he asked, keeping her arms around his neck to keep her balance.

He tugged up the short piece of material that had barely hidden her body and, without wasting another moment, he drove his length inside of her. Pushed deeper with each thrust until he was buried deep within her. He paused for a moment, letting her body adjust to the invasion.

"I've missed this."

"You only want me for the amazing sex," he teased. He kept his arm around her and, with each thrust, her body responded; her inner muscles clamped down on him greedily as he worked his way in and out of her. It didn't take long to find the rhythm that bound them together. Even pressed against the wall, she arched toward him, demanding more. Her heels dug slightly into his back as she tried to meet his thrusts.

"Faster." He didn't need more encouragement. The world narrowed to the pump action of his shaft sliding in and out of her. Nuzzling his neck, she clung to him, her breath coming faster against his collarbone. "Please Kyle…I'm so close."

Burying his face against her neck, his hips slammed against her, every stroke bringing her climax closer. His own just within reach, she exploded around him, her teeth grazing his shoulder as she cried out in pleasure. Her muscles tightened around him and that was all he needed. With a grunt, his body went rigid and he spilled his release inside her. The wave of his orgasm seemed to merge with hers and she shuddered against him with the force of it.

"Amazing," she said breathlessly as she leaned her head against his shoulder. "That doesn't even begin to describe it."

"If you think that was good, just wait until I get you to bed." Not having the energy to move, he kissed her neck.

"Well then." She slipped her legs from his waist. "Let's go."

"You're going to be the death of me," he teased as he let her down from his embrace. "I need some sleep before I can do that again."

"Sleep is for wimps." She stepped away from the wall and headed toward the bedroom.

Watching the way the sheer material clung to her, he could almost agree and say screw sleep. "How's Abbie?" he questioned, following her.

"We have a brand new colt in our stables. He's beautiful, but you can see him tomorrow. Tonight I have other plans for you." She turned back just as she reached the double doors to their room. "Yes, sleep is on the schedule but first you need to tell me why you took a later flight."

The later flight had been so he could spend more time with Johnny and Cassy but when he called to tell her about the change of plans, she had been busy with Abbie so he had to leave a message. Deciding it had been best to tell her in person instead of on her voicemail, he only told her that he had to switch to a later plane. A few hours late had been worth it to spend some extra time with Johnny. The little boy was growing up so quickly, now almost five. Before Kyle would blink, he'd be starting school and become a man. He wished Weber could be there to see his son grow up.

"Kyle?" Staci's voice pulled him back from his thoughts. "Is everything okay?"

"I told you I was going to Weber's grave. Well, I ran into his wife while I was there. She invited me back to the house to see Johnny."

"How did it go?" She moved away from the door and went to the bed. Slipping between the covers, she patted the space next to her.

"Better than I thought it would. Johnny is getting so big and Cassy is doing okay. She's busy with Sewn with Love, so that helps." He slipped out of his clothes, leaving only his boxers on before going to the side of the bed. "I invited them here for a visit. I don't know if they'll come. He'd love the horses but Cassy is terrified something could happen with them."

"That's normal for parents who have no experience with horses."

"I know, and I told her it would be fine. That we have kids here all the time with the horses. So we'll see." He glanced at the picture on the wall of him and Weber a few days before they had deployed.

"Are you okay? You seem…I don't know…different."

"Cassy said that Weber was dead before the IED explosion." He reached down and began to take his prosthetic leg off. "I'm not sure."

"Does it matter?"

He stopped and turned toward her. "Hell yeah. All this time I thought I was the reason he was dead. If I had only left him in the turret he'd be alive; injured like I am, but alive."

"Even if that had been the case, you don't know he'd have survived. He might have given up like you almost did."

"He had a wife and son." He looked away. "I had no one."

"My father had Mom and me and look what happened. Having family there by your side doesn't always make a difference. Maybe for some it makes it worse." She reached out and touched his shoulder. "You had no control over what happened that day, or who lived and died. You're here and call me selfish but I'm thankful for that. I love you, Kyle. I know you lost a good friend and I know he left behind a wife and son, but that isn't your fault. Death finds each of us when it's our time. We have no control over it. No matter how hard you try, you can't cheat death."

With the prosthesis off, he slipped into bed next to her and she cuddled against him. "It's just a shock. I know it doesn't change the fact that Weber is gone but I guess for me it makes a difference." It was stupid but it did bother him. All this time he had blamed himself and now he found out that he wasn't to blame, but it was the insurgent who shot him.

"Tell me about your visit."

He settled in against the pillows, rubbing his hand along her back. "Johnny is a great little boy. He's got three women devoted to his every need."

"Three?"

"Cassy, her sister, and she hired a housekeeper to help with the house and the boy while they are busy with the orders for Sewn with Love." He spent the next few minutes telling her all about the visit with the little guy and the rest of his trip to Colorado. "You know the best part of my trip?"

"What's that?"

"Coming home to you." He kissed the top of her head. "I swear you're more beautiful than when I left."

With her snug beside him, he was finally home. She had once said they were soulmates, completing each other perfectly. He hadn't believed in soulmates before, but as people said, seeing was believing. He was a believer now. She was his everything and those few days apart had left him feeling as though something was missing. Now he had it back. Love really did complete a person.

Chapter Seventeen

It had been a few months since Kyle had come back from the trip to Colorado. The memories that trip provoked had been shoved back into the dark corners of his soul and the nightmares had subsided enough that they were only occasional. Since he had returned it had been nonstop with the ranch and the retreat. Between breeding, training, and racing the horses, he had been busy. Staci and Heather were adjusting to their roles as well. While things had been slow with the retreat, interest had picked up.

Now, Lucky had finished his interview commitments after winning the cook-off and was due at the ranch shortly. This would be the first time they'd have seen each other since the trip and there had been numerous changes in the Gunnery Sergeant's life. The biggest being that he had married Madison and they were expecting their first child in less than a month. Marriage and parenthood for him were no doubt a big change.

He was looking forward to seeing how his Gunny was adjusting to the changes, but something else weighed on his mind about the visit. Weber. He had been putting off asking Lucky or even looking into the cause of Weber's death himself because of what he might find. He had started to accept that it was his fault but the visit with Cassy had given him new hope. Sometime over the next few days, while Lucky was visiting, the truth would finally come out.

"Kyle." Staci stepped out of the house with a tray of iced tea. "There's a truck coming up the drive."

He nodded and looked toward the road. He couldn't see anything except a faint cloud of dust; in order for her to know that, she must have checked the security camera. "They're early, but Lucky was never one to be late."

She sat the tray on the small table on the porch, picked up her phone, and held it out to him. "There's an email I think you should read. I have it up already."

"If it's about purchasing one of the colts, I'll deal with it tonight."

"No." She pushed the phone closer to him. "It's from Cassy Weber."

He glanced at her, hoping to find some hint as to what the email said. This had been the one they were waiting for. The email that would let him know if Cassy and Johnny would be coming for a visit when they made their annual trip to see Weber's ailing mother in Florida. He had been trying to convince her to visit the ranch since he had returned from Colorado, but so far he had no luck.

"Read it," she urged.

Kyle, I've considered this trip for weeks now. Back and forth on whether to come or not. Well, the time is here and a decision needs to be made. While my fear of those big horses around Johnny is still there, my little boy can be adamant and he wants to see you. He wants to go for a horseback ride just like Uncle Kyle promised. We'll be coming, and so there will be no changing my mind. I booked the flight reservations this morning. We're leaving for Florida in two weeks and we'll spend a week there before flying to see you. Johnny is so excited to get there and I'm anxious to meet your wife. See you soon.

"I can't believe it. They're actually coming." The truck could be seen in the distance as he clicked to lock the phone and set it aside. "I wasn't sure she'd agree. I think I owe it all to you. She's coming because you convinced her Johnny would be safe."

"I might have played a role in it." She smirked. "The kid is sweet and there's so much excitement in his voice when he talks to you. I know you care for him and wanted to have them here. So I did what I could."

"Three weeks...that's right around the time when our new guest for the retreat arrives."

"Everything will be fine. Stop worrying and let us enjoy the visit with Gunnery Sergeant Diamond and his new wife Madison."

"I know everything will be fine. Do you know why?" He reached out, wrapped his arm around her waist, and drew her against his body.

"Why?"

"Because I have you. Nothing can go wrong with you by my side." He leaned forward and claimed her lips.

They were still locked in their embrace when the truck pulled up in front of the house, car doors shut, and his Gunny's voice had Kyle cutting the kiss shorter than he'd have liked. "What's all this kissing? We're the ones that are supposed to be newlyweds, not you."

"To keep the spark alive in a relationship you always have to act like newlyweds." She held out her hand. "I'm Staci."

Lucky took it. "Lucky, and this is my wife, Maddie."

"Madison," the pregnant woman beside him corrected. "He's the only one that gets to call me Maddie and live."

"Well, Madison then." She smirked. "It's nice to meet you both. I brought out some fresh iced tea that Josefina made, so why don't we sit down?"

"Actually...umm may I use your restroom? Pregnant woman's bladder and all." Madison blushed as she rubbed a hand over her stomach.

"Sure. Just inside and first door on your right." Staci opened the screen door and pointed to where she meant. "Whenever you need anything, just make yourself at home. I mean..."

"Don't worry, I understand." She hurried off to the bathroom.

"Sugar, Gunny here has never been on a horse." Kyle leaned back in his chair and smirked. He knew he'd just dropped Gunny into it, but it was worth the evil looks he was getting to break the ice between everyone.

"We need to rectify that." She came to stand next to Kyle, her hand on his shoulder. "It's amazing."

"I don't think so." Lucky leaned against the railing, a glass of iced tea in hand. "I've taken enough plunges lately I don't think I need to take any more risks. Sergeant Major Graves is expecting me back on base in a few days and in one piece."

"You'll be in one piece and it will be fun. Another adventure that you can add to your list."

"I think I've had enough adventures lately and at least one more to come. Fatherhood." His eyes widened as if in shock.

"Don't let him fool you." The screen door clicked shut behind Madison. "He's excited to be a father. You should see him with his niece Roulette. When Kyle mentioned the ranch during his trip to Colorado, I told Lucky that we were going to go riding when we visited but with my condition, I can't. Though I still expect you to." She took a seat across from Kyle, her hand instantly going to the top of her stomach.

"We have to get you comfortable around the horses so that after Madison has given birth, you can both come back for a visit and go for a ride," Kyle suggested.

"You'll have to bring the baby," Staci added. "I love babies."

Lucky shook his head. "It might be you two visiting if you want to see our baby. I think Graves is going to have me chained to the base when I finally get back. I've been gone so much with all these interviews and other obligations. I don't think he realized how much it would interfere with things when the two of you recommended me for the cook-off."

"It was for a good cause and you won so he can't bitch. Though I did hear a bunch of Navy SEALs were rooting for you over their own sailor." Kyle chuckled. "Your brother got the whole base revved up and rooting for you."

"He's good at that," Lucky admitted.

They spent the rest of the day catching up, chatting about the good times, while none of them mentioned the mission that had led them all to where they were. The women had even discussed Madison's new work as PR coordinator of her sister-in-law's businesses, Roll of the Diamond and Heart of the Diamond. Everything was perfect until the women wandered inside, leaving Kyle and Lucky alone on the porch.

"I've been waiting until your competition commitments were over, but I can't wait any longer." Kyle looked out over the land, his gaze on Clifford as he led one of the horses into the stables.

"Whatever it is, you've grown serious, so out with it."

"Weber." He took a deep breath and turned to Lucky. "What was the cause of his death?"

"Did you open that envelope?" Lucky shook his head. "Guess not. That day when I came to visit, I left it on your table. It had the paperwork inside. Weber died from the gunshot wound. He was dead before the IED explosion."

"Fuck." He slammed his hand down on the railing. "I threw it away. I didn't care what was in it then and just wanted to die. All this time, I blamed myself."

"I thought you knew or I'd have forced the subject. His widow knows."

"I know," Kyle sighed. "She told me."

"When?"

"Before I caught my flight home from Colorado, I went to finally pay my respects. She was at the cemetery when I was there—the first time I saw her since we deployed. I had been putting it off because I couldn't face her or Johnny. Not after what I *thought* I had done."

"None of what happened was your fault. I'm the one who ordered us on that mission, so if his death is either of our faults it's mine. Widow Weber is doing okay and Johnny, he'll know what kind of man his father was. I've gone to see them and so has Corporal Torres. Just because Weber isn't here doesn't mean we just forget about the family."

"They're coming here. I've been trying to convince Cassy to visit since we reconnected and finally, she's agreed. Johnny's been adamant about visiting the horses. We're going to get him on a horse, too."

"You've turned into a real cowboy. Trying to get everyone else on a horse and everything," Lucky joked. "She's a fighter. She's turned tragedy into something good. Just like you're doing here. United Homefront Ranch, a healing retreat focused on veterans. That's great, I'm proud of you. You were a troubled kid; even after boot camp you let loose a little too much on leave. But you turned into a good Marine and a good man. You're doing something here in memory of those who don't make it back all intact."

Kyle knew it was true and that Cassy would make it through this. He'd make sure of it. Even if he wasn't the cause of Weber's demise, he still owed him and his family that much. Life had thrown poor Cassy a hard blow by taking the man she had been with since they were in high school, leaving her a widow and single mother. Well, Uncle Kyle and Aunt Staci would be there for Johnny and his mother.

Since Staci had walked into his life, things had come full circle. He went from hating he was alive and wanting to die, the guilt just eating at him, to finding out it wasn't pulling Weber into the Humvee that had been the final straw to his death. He was given a second chance at life and he was determined to take advantage of it and live every day to the fullest. He wasn't just living for himself, but he was living also for the life Weber would never have.

Weber, I'll make sure your son knows what kind of man you were. You befriended me when I had no one and made me a part of your family. I'll never forget it. I'll make sure he'll grow up to be just like you. A son that you can be proud of.

Preview: A Marine's Second Chance

Married life hadn't been everything that Wyoming Dorset dreamed of. She thought she knew what she was getting into when she fell in love with a Marine. Training and deployments were the least of their problems. What she couldn't deal with was the distance that Jeffrey put between them. Only a shell of the man she fell in love with stood before her.

Five years—that's how long they'd been married. As Jeffrey prepared for another deployment, he thought of Wyoming and wondered how much of their marriage he'd been there for. How much had he been gone for? The divide between them seemed to appear overnight and now he wasn't sure how to fix it.

When unexpected news arrived hours before his deployment, somehow he convinced her to give him a second chance. She doesn't know why, but he believes that even with miles separating them, he can convince her that they haven't lost their chance. She's not sure if she believes him, but he'll be back in six months. That isn't too long to wait for her husband.

Chapter One

Pregnant? Wyoming Dorset sat there staring at her husband, waiting for him to say something. Saying anything would be better than silence. This would have been happy news if it was earlier in their marriage, but now…now she didn't know. Their marriage was on shaky ground, and the wall he threw up between them became thicker with every deployment. How did this happen? They had taken precautions. She was on the pill, never missing a day even when he was gone, because she never knew when he'd return.

"Damn it, Jeffrey, say something." She couldn't take the silence any longer. If he was angry, then she wanted him to rage. If he was happy about the pregnancy, she needed to hear it. Whatever was going through his mind, she needed to know because the silence was torture.

"I…" He dropped his bag on the bed. "How far along are you?"

"Don't you dare, Jeffrey! You might not give a shit about me or this child, but don't you dare ask me to have—"

"Is that what you think? That I don't care about you?" In a quick stride he came around the bed and touched the side of her face, caressing her cheek. "Damn it, Wyoming, that couldn't be further from the truth."

"You have a funny way of showing it." She fought against the instinct to press against his hand and enjoy the sweet caress. How long had it been since he'd touched her like that? How long had it been since the romance left their relationship? She could pinpoint the date and time she noticed the first change in him, but how had she let it get so bad?

"Wyoming, I—"

This time, she cut him off. She couldn't take one more excuse, or another one of his halfhearted apologies. "It doesn't matter. Things changed and we're just too different now. It's too late, but please don't ask me to have an abortion. Let me hold on to some respect for you." She took a deep breath because the moment she feared was there in front of her, and nothing could stop the outcome. "You don't have to worry about it. We'll be gone when you get back."

"Fuck!" Dropping his hand away from her cheek, he took a step back.

The absence of his touch made her heart ache. Even after everything, she still loved him. Tears pricked behind her eyelids, and she blinked them away. There was plenty of time for tears later, but she refused to cry in front of him. She didn't want him to stay out of pity, or because of the pregnancy. Love and romance, that's what she wanted.

He stepped back farther until the back of his legs brushed along the edge of the bed and he sat down, letting out a deep sigh. "That's not what I want. Abortion never crossed my mind."

"Then why ask how far along I am?" Maybe she jumped to a conclusion without giving him a chance, but it was the first thing that popped into her thoughts.

"It's September. If you conceived six weeks ago, that would be July." He glanced up at her, the corners of his lips pulling into a smile. "Everyone in my family who got pregnant in July had a girl. But if you're further along..."

"Nine weeks, but it will be a few weeks before we know the sex."

"Stay." He shot off the bed and came to stand in front of her. "Don't leave. This mission shouldn't take long, and I'll be back soon."

"I don't know." She wanted him to wrap his arms around her and tell her that everything would be fine. It wasn't that simple, especially not between them. She had a stable career, and she could provide for her and the child if he wasn't in the picture. Would she have considered leaving him if a child wasn't involved? She wasn't sure. Their relationship had been shaky for more than a year but she hadn't thought of divorce until she found out she was pregnant. There was no way she wanted to raise a child in a house filled with the tension that surrounded them. *I'm doing this for you, little one.* But was it the right thing?

"Even if you don't anymore, at one time you loved me," he said. "We owe it to our child to find that love again." He took her hand in his and dragged his thumb across her wedding band. "My feelings for you haven't changed. They're still the same as the day I put this on your finger. I know I haven't been the best husband, but let me prove to you that I want you in my life. I can be the man you need me to be. I can be the father to our daughter that she deserves. Don't give up on me."

"We've got to go, you need to be at—"

"Screw it," he snapped. "Damn it, Wyoming. I love you. I'm an asshole and I don't deserve you, but that doesn't mean I don't want you."

Tears filled her eyes and this time she couldn't blink them away. She wanted things to be different, but wasn't it too late for them? Did they have a chance to fix whatever was broken between them? Could they do it before the baby was born? She wanted her child to grow up surrounded by love.

"Don't cry, baby." He wrapped his arms around her and pulled her tight against his chest. "I never wanted to be the reason you cry. If you don't love me, I'll support your decision but—"

"Damn it, Jeffrey." Tears came faster and her chest tightened. "Loving you was never the problem. I've always loved you."

"Then stay." He loosened his embrace and leaned back so that she could look at him. "Give me time to prove to you that I can be the man you need, and a good father to our child. We'll make this right. Give me a chance."

"It's not always that easy." She took him in and tried to decide if he was willing to listen to her, or if he'd shut her out again and close off communication like he always did when she tried to talk to him about something like this. "There's a wall between us now, and every time I try to breach it, you reinforce it. We never even talk anymore. You always made me laugh but now…" *There's only tears.* She couldn't bring herself to say the last part. It wasn't only his fault. Maybe she could have done something different, something to get him to open up to her.

"Give me another chance." He cupped the side of her face, brushing his thumb along her cheek, wiping away the tears. "The man who made you laugh is still there, just buried, but I can find him again. This deployment is short. I'll be back before you know it and I'll prove it to you. Stay, baby."

She wanted to believe him. She wanted the man she fell in love with back again. Was it possible? She didn't know, but she was willing to give it a chance. Maybe she was clinging to her dream of the perfect family, but she believed their son or daughter deserved to have both parents. She wanted the happy family home she'd envied as a child. A mother and father who actually got along, the two and a half kids, and the white picket fence. "I'll be here when you get back." She could give him that long and see how things went.

"Promise?"

"Yes." She met his gaze and nodded. After five years of marriage, they deserved this chance. She wasn't willing to throw away all their time together, their memories, and the love she had for him if he was willing to try. "Now, we should get on the road."

"I promise you're not going to regret this decision." He pulled her back against him. "I love you, Wyoming. Things are going to be different, I promise."

She wrapped her arms around him, returning his embrace. How long had it been since they shared an embrace like that? In her gut, she knew the answer—just before he'd deployed a year ago. Just before the change in him.

Since then, any time they held each other, it was short and his body felt stiff. He closed her out. Maybe he'd do it again, but she had to give him the benefit of the doubt that this time would be different. "I love you, too."

Chapter Two

The volunteer deployment had seemed like the perfect opportunity when Jeffrey agreed, but he hadn't realized how much his life would change just hours before he shipped out. Six months seemed like nothing when he signed the paperwork, but now that Wyoming was pregnant it felt like an eternity. He had so much to prove to her, and the distance between them would only make that harder.

Until the words came out of her mouth that she would be gone before he got back, he hadn't realized how close he came to losing her. She was everything to him. Before boarding his flight, he clung to her longer than normal, reminding himself that she'd be there when he returned. This wasn't goodbye. Six months...he'd be back before the birth of their child. Now that the plane was in the air, he couldn't shake the weight on his shoulders or the knot in his gut. Maybe he was overthinking things, but his gut told him that this deployment wasn't going to be a walk in the park. He'd have to fight hard to make it back to her. *If I make it back to her...no, when I make it back...I'm done.*

His commitment to the Marines was up in ten months and he wasn't reenlisting. Before he found out that she was pregnant, he had planned to. It was why he volunteered for this deployment. Advancement in his career. Becoming a father would change things. He wanted to be there to see his child grow and he didn't want to miss all the things his own father missed while he was growing up. No, Jeffrey wanted to be there when his child took his first steps, said his or her first word, and he wanted to be there with Wyoming. They'd find a way through the darkness that had surrounded him since he returned from his last deployment.

He was willing to admit to himself, if to no one else, that his last deployment changed him. Something snapped within him and what he saw overseas plagued his dreams. Too many of his buddies were injured or dead due to bad intelligence. How he'd managed to walk away unharmed was something he couldn't understand.

He made it home to Wyoming because of Gunnery Sergeant Lucky Diamond. They drove right into a trap, but Lucky got them out alive. Most of them, but not everyone, made it. Memories of that mission filled his thoughts as he leaned back against the airplane seat.

Gunfire broke out in nearly every direction and they were sitting ducks in the middle of the road. He was taking in the situation, looking for possible routes to keep them alive, when Gunnery Sergeant Diamond's voice crackled over the radio. "Reverse. Fall back. Now!"

With another Humvee behind them, he hoped they heard the orders and their escape hadn't been closed off. As soon as he had the clearance, he swung left and turned the Humvee around, gunning it back the way they came, with the third Humvee in their caravan now leading the way. They were taking some gunfire, but the insurgents seemed to be focusing more on Lucky's Humvee, which had been the lead vehicle. One minute the gunshots were deafening, and then the next the assault subsided. Johnson's machinegun fired the only continuing shots.

Had they won? Was it winning if they were retreating to safer grounds? No, it was living to fight another day. He pressed his foot against the pedal a little harder, hoping to put more distance between them. They needed to get somewhere safe and regroup. The battle was ending but the war wasn't over. Regrouping…

A bomb exploded, shaking the road under his wheels and for the moment he had to make sure he hadn't run over an IED. It wasn't until he checked the mirror that he realized what happened. Gunny's Humvee sailed through the air for what seemed like an eternity before landing on its side with a thump, thirty feet from where it had been. Something else sailed through the air. What was it?

"Fuck!" Johnson hollered from the turret, where he was returning fire.

There was no doubt in his mind that Johnson had seen the same thing. One of their comrades had been thrown from the Humvee, to land hard, and now wasn't moving. Whoever it was might not be alive but they had to do something.

"Dorset!" Doc, their corpsman, dug into his field bag, preparing to respond.

"I know." Jeffrey slammed his foot down on the break. "Johnson, watch our backs and shoot anything that moves."

He grabbed his rifle from the rack near the door hinge and headed to assist. Doc needed to patch up whoever was still alive and they needed to get out of there before the insurgents opened fired on them again.

"Shit, it's Phillips." Even from this distance he could recognize Private First Class Phillips. Blood spilled along the sand, coming faster than it could be absorbed, making him wonder if Phillips was even alive.

With a jerk of his head, Jeffrey let go of the memories, but he couldn't shake the images of Kyle Phillips's mangled body. The young Private First Class had been new to their unit and with his presence he brought a new ray of hope. He was lighthearted and happy-go-lucky, something the whole unit needed.

Refusing to allow the memories of the last deployment to set the tone for this one, he turned his thoughts to his wife and unborn child. If he had to, he'd fight harder to make it home to them. He was going to be there when his child was born, and he wouldn't be like his absent father. He'd be in their life from the beginning, never missing an event, and making sure they knew he was always there if they needed him. He'd prove to Wyoming that the love they shared was still there and strong. *How? I don't know, but I'll do it.*

The first day of a deployment always seemed to be the hardest for Wyoming. Other wives felt the opposite, that they could picture their spouse on duty, so the first day wasn't as difficult. That it was later in the deployments that things became harder. For her, the minute she walked through the front door of their house, it sank in that it was the first of many days she'd be alone.

She sank down on the sofa and stared up at their wedding picture. It was a simple affair with a justice of the peace marrying them in a nearby park. Their parents, her sister, and a couple friends were there to witness their special day. Everything was so perfect, giving her the hope it would always be that way.

"I miss the way things used to be." She grabbed the throw pillow and hugged it to her chest, thinking of the early days of their marriage when he returned home at the end of the day and they couldn't keep their hands off each other. The sex had always been good, but back then they'd cuddle in bed or on the sofa as they watched a movie. Now he sat in the recliner, leaving her alone on the sofa. In bed, he stuck to his side of the mattress and kept his back to her. The lines between them were drawn firmly, making her doubt that things would be different when he returned.

Our parents. Dread settled over her shoulders. With him gone, she was left to tell them the news of her pregnancy alone. Having family get-togethers were never the highlight of her day. They always seemed to turn into a disaster as her parents couldn't even stand to be in the same room together, let alone get through a whole meal peacefully. Her mother-in-law didn't make the situation easier by butting in with her comments about how she'd never put up with the way Wyoming's father treated her mother. Halfway through dinner, she was ready to scream for everyone to get out, but Jeffrey always had a way of keeping the situation under control.

"Maybe I can video chat them?" She wasn't sure it was the best way to tell them, but it certainly was the least stressful. Before she had time to consider it further, her cell phone beeped, alerting her to a text.

Come for dinner? 6? I'll chill the wine. Her best friend Alessa, already reminding her that she wasn't alone. Both military spouses, they stuck together when their husbands deployed. Being in the same unit, they were normally gone together, giving her peace of mind knowing that Jeffrey had someone watching his back. It also kept her from feeling like a third wheel.

Needing to be alone, she shot back a quick text. *Thanks, but another night. I'm tired. Lunch tomorrow—usual place.*

Before she could set her phone down, a reply came through. *See you then.*

With a smile, she put the phone aside and stretched out on the sofa. Before she told their parents or her sister, she'd tell Alessa. Even though Alessa and Steve had been trying to get pregnant for the last two years, she knew her best friend would be happy for them. *Happier than my parents.*

MARISSA DOBSON

Born and raised in the Pittsburgh, Pennsylvania area, Marissa Dobson now resides about an hour from Washington, D.C. She's a lady who likes to keep busy, and is always busy doing something. With two different college degrees, she believes you're never done learning.

Being the first daughter to an avid reader, this gave her the advantage of learning to read at a young age. Since learning to read she has always had her nose in a book. It wasn't until she was a teenager that she started writing down the stories she came up with.

Marissa is blessed with a wonderful supportive husband, Thomas. He's her other half and allows her to stay home and pursue her writing. He puts up with all her quirks and listens to her brainstorm in the middle of the night.

Her writing buddy Pup Cameron, a cocker spaniel, is always around to listen to her bounce ideas off him. He might not be able to answer, but he's helpful in his own ways.

She loves to hear from readers so send her an email at marissa@marissadobson.com or visit her online at http://www.marissadobson.com.

OTHER BOOKS BY MARISSA DOBSON

Alaskan Tigers:

Tiger Time

The Tiger's Heart

Tigress for Two

Night with a Tiger

Trusting a Tiger

Alaskan Tigers Box Set Vol. 1

Jinx's Mate

Two for Protection

Bearing Secrets

Tiger Tracks

Healing the Clan

Alaskan Tigers Box Set Vol. 2

Her Black Tiger

Tiger Troubl

Alpha Claimed

Forever Creek Shifters:

Forever's Fight

Protecting Forever

Stormkin:

Storm Queen

Crimson Hollow:

Romancing the Fox

Loving the Bears

A Lion's Chance

Swift Move

Purrable Lion

Bearly Alive

Saved by a Lion

Furever Mated Box Set

Reaper:

A Touch of Death

SEALed for You:

Ace in the Hole

Explosive Passion

Operation Family

Marine for You:

Lucky Chance

Back from Hell

A Marine's Second Chance

United Homefront Ranch:

Destination Heaven

Tanner Cycles:

Until Sydney

Phantom Security:

Different Sides

Undercover Agent

Cedar Grove Medical:

Hope's Toy Chest

Destiny's Wish

Leena's Dream

Fate:

Snowy Fate

Sarah's Fate

Mason's Fate

As Fate Would Have It

Half Moon Harbor Resort:

Learning to Live

Learning What Love Is

Her Cowboy's Heart

Half Moon Harbor Resort Vol. 1

Beyond Monogamy:

Theirs to Treasure

Clearwater:

Winterbloom

Unexpected Forever

Losing to Win

Christmas Countdown

The Surrogate

Clearwater Romance Volume One

Small Town Doctor

Stand Alone:

Through Smoke

SEALed Rescue

SEALed in Texas

Starting Over

Secret Valentine

Restoring Love

www.ingramcontent.com/pod-product-compliance
Lightning Source LLC
Chambersburg PA
CBHW030301130626
46549CB00002B/642